Black Holes and Uncle Albert

*by the same author*

**THE TIME AND SPACE OF UNCLE ALBERT**

# BLACK HOLES
# AND
# UNCLE ALBERT

## Russell Stannard

illustrations by John Levers

*faber and faber*

LONDON · BOSTON

First published in 1991
by Faber and Faber Limited
3 Queen Square London WC1N 3AU

Photoset by Parker Typesetting Service Leicester
Printed in England by Clays Ltd St Ives plc

A CIP record for this book
is available from the British Library

ISBN 0571 16199 5

2 4 6 8 10 9 7 5 3

My thanks

– to the children of Linslade Middle School
  and Brooklands School, Leighton Buzzard, for
  kindly sharing with me their thoughts about
  time, space and the Universe
– to David Broadhurst for helpful comments on
  the physics
– and to my wife, Maggi, for her encouragement.

Russell Stannard

# Contents

# Prologue

*The greedy black hole was all set to devour its victim. There was no going back now. She knew she shouldn't have done it. 'Under NO circumstances get too close to it,' Uncle Albert had warned.*

*Gedanken's body was gripped by intense gravity forces. She was being stretched out as on a torture rack – her feet felt they were being ripped off from the rest of her body. A crushing weight bore down on her chest; she could hardly breathe. The walls of the spacecraft strained and creaked. With a screeching metallic scraping noise, they began to buckle inwards. The complete rocket section of the craft tore away.*

*Yet even now, Gedanken had not completely lost hope. Fighting back her tears, she muttered defiantly through clenched teeth, 'Come on, Uncle. I know you can do it.'*

*So she braced herself for the final moment. The end of a marvellous journey of discovery – an adventure that had started so innocently the afternoon she and Uncle Albert had gone to the fairground . . .*

# 1 Something Very Fishy

'Brilliant!' exclaimed Gedanken, emerging from the exit to the Big Dipper, her face flushed with excitement. 'You should have come.'

'Huh!' snorted Uncle Albert. 'At my age?'

'Chicken!'

Gedanken was having a great time. She loved the fair. Her uncle had suggested they go as a bank holiday treat. She only hoped that he was enjoying it too, even though he didn't want to go on anything.

'What was it like?' asked Uncle Albert.

'Great. But my tummy felt *awful*.'

'So you don't want any of that candy floss stuff over there?'

Her eyes widened. 'No, no,' she said hastily. 'It's all right now. Fine. Fine.'

Candy floss was one of her favourites. Why was it you only got it at places like fairs and the seaside? One day she would make a fortune selling it everywhere.

Gratefully she took hold of the stick and started tucking in. 'Like a bit?'

She pulled off a fluffy piece and with sticky

fingers offered it to Uncle Albert. He took it – rather as you might pick up a worm in the garden – and popped it gingerly in his mouth. One munch and a swallow. 'Load of nothing if you ask me,' he grunted.

They carried on walking round the side-shows. In between mouthfuls, Gedanken resumed,

'The really frightening part was when you got to the top and suddenly started going down. You felt you were drifting out of your seat. Then at the bottom of that big drop, it was like crashing through the seat into the ground. My tummy dropped into my bottom. I felt so heavy I could hardly sit up properly.'

Uncle Albert started to chuckle.

'What's so funny?' asked Gedanken.

'Your nose. It's on your nose.'

Gedanken went cross-eyed. She caught a glimpse of pink. With her eyes still crossed, she stuck her tongue out and tried to curl it upwards. It didn't quite reach.

Uncle Albert laughed. 'Oh for a camera.' Then he added, '*Stop it*, for goodness sake. Your face'll get stuck.'

'Wouldn't. That's stupid. You don't get stuck just because you pull a face.'

They stopped to watch the dodgems. The owner was angrily shouting at some boys to stop bumping the cars deliberately. Gedanken told Uncle Albert she knew one of the boys from school. His name was Jeremy. He was *always* getting into trouble.

4

She carried on chattering away happily for a while before she realized that Uncle Albert wasn't saying much. She looked at him.

'Anything the matter?'

'Mmmm?' asked Uncle Albert absent-mindedly.

'You all right?' she asked.

'Yes, fine. Why shouldn't I be?'

'Nothing. It's just that you weren't saying a lot.'

'I was thinking.'

'What about?'

'What you said back there.'

'That boy at the dodgems? Or your face not getting stuck . . .?'

'No, not that. No, I was thinking about feeling heavy when you got to the bottom of that drop and started going up again – and feeling light and floaty at the top.'

'So?'

'Nothing. It's just that feeling light or heavy is all to do with gravity. It's *gravity* that pulls you down and presses you to the floor. But what you're saying is that when you accelerate – when you go faster and faster in an upwards direction – as you did coming out of that big drop – it's like adding extra gravity. And going in the opposite direction – falling – is like switching gravity off.'

'Pretty obvious, if you ask me.'

'Yes. Yes, I suppose so. It's just that I've never seriously thought about it before. Now that I do . . . well, I don't know . . . seems sort of odd somehow. Anyway,' he said, looking around him, 'had enough?'

'Not yet. One more go, please,' she pleaded.

'Well, I don't know. I'm almost out,' he said examining his loose change. 'Could just about manage one more, I suppose. All right, what shall it be?'

She thought for a moment, and then decided: 'The Whiplash.'

'The *what*?'

'The Whiplash. The one over there,' said Gedanken pointing. 'That big arm with the cabins on the ends. It whirls you round and round, and you get pressed into your seats, and you scream and scream, and pretend to be frightened and you hope you're sitting next to a boy . . .'

Back at Uncle Albert's, Gedanken searched the fridge for a Coke; he made himself a coffee. She couldn't find one, so had to settle for an orange juice. They took their drinks through to the study, he settling into his well-worn leather armchair, she squatting on the floor beside him.

For a while they said nothing. Gedanken wondered whether anyone ever fell off the Big Dipper. Uncle Albert reached across for the newspaper. She thought he was going to read it, but instead he tore a piece off the corner. Out of his pocket he pulled a bunch of keys. With the bit of paper in one hand and the keys in the other, he held his arms straight out in front of him at the same height. He opened both hands. The keys crashed to the floor next to

Gedanken; the piece of paper followed, slowly fluttering from side to side like a snowflake.

'Hey! Watch it!' cried Gedanken.

He looked at them thoughtfully. 'Funny thing, gravity. Why do you think that happened?' he asked.

'What do you think! You let go of them. I saw you . . .'

'But why did the keys fall faster than the paper?'

'Because they're heavier, of course.'

'Ye-es,' said Uncle Albert. 'They're certainly that. But there's something else going on here. Take another look. Keep your eye on the paper.'

As it fluttered down again he said, 'There! Why is it doing *that*?'

'Going from side to side, you mean?'

'Yes.'

'Dunno.'

'Air resistance. It's having to push its way through the air.'

'But so do the keys,' said Gedanken.

'Yes, but it's easier for the keys. As you said, they're heavier. So they punch their way through. The paper is light; it doesn't pack a punch. It has to nudge its way through.' He sat back. 'Now the question is – what if there were *no* air? What would happen then? What would gravity on its own do?'

'What *are* you on about, Uncle? What's the point?'

'The point? The point is that acceleration can fake gravity. That's what you spotted on the Big Dipper.

Now, no other force can be faked.' He reached out towards her and pressed his hand firmly down on her head.

'Hey! Stop that!' yelled Gedanken indignantly.

She sprang to her feet and went to look in the mirror in the hall. 'Oh, NO,' she cried, taking a comb out. 'Took me ages to get that right.' She carefully straightened out the spikes.

'Sorry,' said Uncle Albert when she returned. 'Just trying to make a point.'

'What point?' she muttered grumpily.

'Just that ordinary forces – normal pushes and pulls – they can't be faked. They can't be faked by simply changing your motion, or anything like that. Just now, when I pushed down on you, you knew straight away what was happening – there was a force of some kind. But with gravity – you can't be sure. On the Dipper, if you had your eyes shut and your ears plugged up – so you couldn't see or hear what was going on – and you just thought about how heavy or light you felt, and what was happening to your tummy – you wouldn't know for sure what was happening. It could be that you were suddenly changing your motion, or it might be that an extra force of gravity had been switched on. You can't tell. Now, that's odd. Very odd. A force that comes and goes depending on your motion. I reckon something funny's going on. We need to know more about it.'

'How are you going to do that?'

'Well, first we've got to get rid of air resistance –

so we can see exactly what gravity itself is doing.'
He leant forward and picked up the bunch of keys
and the bit of paper. 'And that means dropping
these things where there is no air,' adding with a
knowing look, 'like, for example – on the Moon.'

Gedanken was suddenly all attention. The hurt
look vanished and she promptly forgot about her
hair. Her eyes widened. 'You mean . . .'

He nodded.

She squealed with delight. Springing up, she
threw her arms round his neck. Then she flopped
down in the chair opposite. 'Mission controller!
Beam me up!'

At this point you need to know that Gedanken
and her uncle shared a special secret. Uncle Albert
was a famous scientist. He did most of his work by
thinking very hard. He got so good at it he could
actually produce a thought-bubble! It was like those
you get in comics – over people's heads when they
are having a thought – only this one was a bit more
real. That in itself was remarkable. Even more amazing was his ability to beam Gedanken up into this
thought world. If he thought of a spacecraft, for
example, then Gedanken would find herself in a
spacecraft! Many had been the voyages of discovery
she had made in this – the most powerful spacecraft
that had never been built, and never will be.

So it was that Uncle Albert closed his eyes, rested
his chin on his hand, and began to have a Big Think.
In a short while, a hazy, fuzzy patch appeared
above his head. Gradually it took shape. It looked

like a large, wobbling soap bubble. As Gedanken peered into the bubble she began to make out the spacecraft.

'It's there, Uncle,' she said excitedly. 'I can see the spacecraft. I'm ready when you are.'

'Hold on, hold on. You have to take these with you.' Uncle Albert slowly held out the keys and the piece of paper, trying not to disturb his concentration.

She took them. 'What do I have to do?' she whispered.

'Exactly what I did. Hold them at the same height above the ground and let go of them both at the same moment. Tell me what happens.'

'That's all?'

He nodded.

As Gedanken stared intently into the bubble the spacecraft got clearer and clearer. It was very big with curved walls and round windows. There was an important-looking control desk with winking lights and switches and TV monitors. Soon it was right in front of her. It looked close enough to touch. She reached out. With a thrill she felt its hard metallic surface. She quickly looked about her. The outline of the bubble had disappeared. Mysteriously she had been transported *into* the bubble – and not only into the bubble, but also into the spacecraft. The first time this had happened to her, she had been scared to death. But now she thought nothing of it.

'Hi, Dick!' she called out merrily. 'It's me.'

'Welcome aboard, Captain,' said the talking computer. 'Good to have you with us again. It's been quite a while.'

'Been busy – this and that, you know.'

'Well, actually I *wouldn't* know – being *just* a computer. You humans seem to forget it's *you* that have all the fun. You can get about on those leg things of yours; we have to stay where you put us. You have no idea how boring it is to be a computer. Especially for me, having to hang around waiting for Uncle Albert to think me back into existence.'

'Well, if you didn't exist since I was last here, you *couldn't* have been bored.'

'Boredom gets into *everything*. There is nothing *more* boring than not existing.'

Gedanken thought for a moment. She was fairly sure that didn't make sense, but wasn't prepared to argue. Her parents were always telling *her* off for going on about things being boring. She was actually very fond of Dick, but he did have his moods.

'Right,' she said decisively. 'Let's be on our way.'

'Where to?'

'The Moon.'

'That all? It's just round the corner. Not worth starting up the motors. Let's go somewhere more interesting.'

'I *like* the Moon, if you must know. We can go somewhere else another day. We've got to obey orders – you know that. If Uncle Albert says the Moon, then the Moon it is.'

'Why can't you think for yourself sometimes?'

'That sounds great coming from a p-r-o-g-r-a-m-m-e-d computer!'

She strapped herself into her seat. 'Set course, Dick – to the MOON,' she added firmly.

'Oh, very well,' replied the computer. 'Do this, do that, always the same . . .'

Gedanken pressed the big red button on the control panel in front of her. Immediately the rocket motors roared into life, drowning the sound of Dick's complaints.

It wasn't long before they landed on the Moon. Dick reminded her to wear her spacesuit outside – because of the lack of any atmosphere. It looked bulky, but was well designed, and not too awkward to wear. Through the air lock she went, down the metal steps, and out on to the Moon's dusty surface. For a while she played about, jumping up and down. She loved the way she could jump much higher than on the Earth. 'Must be what it's like to be an Olympic jumper,' she thought.

'Ahem,' came a voice from inside her helmet. 'Is that all you have to do?' It was the radio link to Dick in the craft.

'No,' replied Gedanken. 'Just about to get started. I have to do an experiment.' She rummaged in her pockets and pulled out the keys with one hand, and the bit of paper with the other. 'I've got to let go of them and see what happens. Waste of time really. They'll just float. Like this.' With that she opened the hand holding the keys. They fell to the ground.

'Oh,' said Gedanken in some surprise.

'Float? Why float?' came Dick's voice.

'Because we're out in space, and there's no gravity . . .' Her voice trailed off uncertainly.

'Shouldn't let Uncle Albert hear you say that.'

'Why not?'

'Well, *you* aren't floating off into space, are you? What do you think's holding *you* down? What brought you back down to the ground when you jumped just now? Gravity. The *Moon*'s gravity. It's not as strong as the Earth's; the Earth is heavier. That's why you jumped higher. But it's still gravity.'

Gedanken felt like kicking herself. It was obvious – once you thought about it. 'How did *you* know that, Dick?'

'It's in my memory somewhere. I have to know that sort of thing otherwise I wouldn't know how hard to fire the retro-rockets to give you a gentle landing. Anyway, have you finished? Is that it?'

'No, no. I've got to drop the keys and this bit of paper at the same time.' Having picked up the keys, she held her arms out wide, with the keys in one hand and the piece of paper in the other. She looked from one to the other to make sure they were at the same height. Then she opened both hands at the same moment. She watched the keys fall, noting that they fell more slowly than they would have done on the Earth. The instant they landed, she glanced across at the paper. She expected it to be still fluttering down. But it wasn't. It was already on the ground. She was puzzled. Had it slipped out of her hand earlier without her noticing? It was awfully fiddly with gloves on. She picked up both the paper and the keys, and this time held her arms out immediately in front of her – where she could keep her eye on both at the same time. Again she released them. To her astonishment, they fell together. Both landed at exactly the same moment! The paper

didn't flutter about from side to side; it just went straight down. She repeated the experiment several times. There was no doubt about it. The motion of the keys and the paper was the same. What this meant she couldn't imagine. But she was pretty sure Uncle Albert would find it interesting.

On the way back to Earth, they were just about to begin their final descent when Gedanken saw a flash of light in the distance. 'What was that, Dick?'

'What was what?'

'Thought I saw a flash – over there,' she said, pointing out of the window.

'That? Must have been the American Space Shuttle. It's due in orbit over there sometime now. Probably caught a reflection of the Sun.'

'Ooh, could we take a closer look?'

'Don't see why not.' With that, Dick changed course, and in a short while they came up from behind the Shuttle.

'Switch off engine,' Dick commanded, and she let go the red button. In silence the two craft coasted alongside each other; they were very close.

After a while, Dick had an idea. 'Fancy a space walk? You've never done one, have you?'

'A space walk!' exclaimed Gedanken. She shivered at the thought. 'No thank you. I wouldn't know how.'

'Nothing to it really. You put your spacesuit on, strap on a personal rocket pack, and attach a rope so you don't go drifting off.'

'No thank you,' repeated Gedanken firmly.

'As you wish,' said Dick.

Suddenly, there was a peculiar clucking, squawking type of noise. Gedanken was startled. 'What was that?'

'That,' said Dick mischievously, 'was a computer's attempt to imitate a chicken.'

'I'm *not* chicken,' said Gedanken angrily. 'It's just that . . . well . . . We don't have time for it.'

'We've plenty of time,' said Dick. 'Seriously, I think you'd enjoy it.'

Gedanken thought for a moment. Then, screwing up her courage, she declared, 'Oh, all right. What do I have to do?' She donned the spacesuit and rocket pack. Dick explained that to move about in space you have to use little rockets or jets. When fired you got pushed in the opposite direction to that in which the jet was squirting out. By directing the jet, you could control the direction in which you went. She clipped the rope on to a hook attached to her suit, and made sure that the other end was securely fastened to a hook on the wall of the air lock. Gripping a hand rail, she waited for the door of the air lock to open. As soon as it did, the air rushed out of the compartment, and the flight of steps automatically extended out beyond the craft. Only now they went nowhere! There wasn't any ground or anything to walk on at the end!

The surface of the Earth was a hundred miles or so away.

'If I fall from this height . . .' she thought to herself. Yet the funny thing was she didn't feel as though she would fall. She was floating – in the same way as the keys *didn't* when she released them on the Moon. 'Perhaps *this* is where there is no gravity. It's all very muddly.'

Gingerly she let go. She gently floated out of the hatch, trailing the rope behind her. So far so good. Now to try the rocket jets. At first she went all over the place, this way and that, and then into a spin. But eventually she got the hang of it. It was a matter of learning how to direct the little jets.

For a while she was content to float and slowly tumble in space admiring the view of the Earth below her – or was it above her? Then she got the idea of going across to the American Shuttle. She reckoned the rope had just enough slack in it to allow her to reach it. On arriving, she worked her way round to the front window. Peering in, she could see one of the astronauts. He was reading a book. At first he didn't notice her. So she tapped on the window. You should have seen the look of horror! The poor fellow thought he had come face to face with an alien.

Gedanken was still laughing when she got back to Uncle Albert's study, having been beamed down.

'All right, all right,' her uncle interrupted. 'Glad you had a good time, but did you do the experiment?'

'Yes,' said Gedanken, 'and you'll never guess the result.'

'Well, go on.'

'They arrived at the same time!'

'The keys and the bit of paper?'

'Yep. Exactly at the same time.'

'Good.'

'Good? What do you mean "good"? Aren't you surprised?'

'Not really. I had a hunch it might turn out like that. But it's good to be sure. By the way,' he added in a knowing manner, 'what's all this I hear about there being no gravity on the Moon?'

'Dick had no business telling you that,' Gedanken said crossly.

'Oh, it doesn't matter. We all make mistakes. Best way to learn. So, what *did* you learn – from that experiment of yours?'

'Well . . .' she ventured. 'The Moon has a gravity, and things fall on the Moon. But it is not as strong as gravity on the Earth – because the Moon is smaller and lighter. And the keys and the paper fall exactly the same way.'

'Correct.'

'But, Uncle, I don't understand. Gravity works on the surface of the Earth or the Moon, and it still works just off the surface, so as to pull things down on to it. But it doesn't work in space, right?'

'What do you mean – "space"?'

'Where the Shuttle was. Where I was doing the space walk. We were just floating. We didn't fall or anything. We just stayed put where we were.'

'No, you didn't.'

'We did,' insisted Gedanken.

'But you didn't. You were in orbit, remember. You were going round the Earth in orbit – in a circle.'

'So?'

'Well, normally we expect things to go in straight lines. If you were right out in empty space – I mean a long, long way from anything else – you'd expect to go straight ahead. But you went in a *circle*. So, there must have been a force acting on you – sideways – to keep pulling you round.'

'Gravity? You're saying the Earth's gravity was pulling us?'

'Yes. It's the same as that Whiplash thing you went on. The cabin went whirling around in a circle. Why? Because of the force in the arm. If the link between the cabin and the arm broke . . .'

'It would fly off,' suggested Gedanken.

'Exactly. So, no more talk about there not being gravity up there. It's gravity that kept you in orbit – you and the Shuttle. Come to think of it,' he added, 'that was very daring of you – that space walk of yours. I wouldn't have had the nerve.'

'Oh, there was nothing to it, really,' she said, secretly pleased that she could do something her uncle couldn't.

Uncle Albert rose and started pacing up and down. 'Actually that space walk of yours was very interesting,' he said. 'The two of you – the Shuttle and you – floating together, side by side, in the same orbit. The Shuttle much heavier than you. Yet going in the *same* orbit. That means gravity had to pull harder on it – harder than on you – to keep it in that orbit. But how come? How did it *know* how much harder it had to pull? In any case, why should it *want* the two of you in the same orbit?'

'Has this got anything to do with the keys and the paper?' asked Gedanken. 'Gravity knew how much harder it had to pull on the keys – to make them hit the ground at the same time as the paper. Is that the same kind of thing?'

'Hey, you're right. Dead right. Yes, keys and paper – Shuttles and space walkers – they're all being steered through space and time in the same way by gravity. Start the keys and paper at rest at the same place – the same height above the Moon's surface – and they arrive together at the ground at the same time. Start a Shuttle and a space walker off in the same direction and at the same speed, and they stay together following exactly the same path round the Earth. Why? Why does gravity do this? It's all much too fishy for my liking.'

At this point in Uncle Albert's path around his study he reached the fireplace and caught sight of the clock on the mantlepiece. 'Good Heavens. Is that the time? I promised to have you back by now. Your parents will be sending out search parties. Off you go.'

'But it was just getting interesting,' protested Gedanken.

'A visit to the Moon and a space walk – to say nothing of the Big Dipper and the Whiplash – all in one day? Come now, that's enough. We'll carry on with this another time.'

'But when?'

'Oh . . . I don't know. Friday. Yes, let's say Friday – after school.'

As he saw her to the door, he felt in his pockets. 'My keys!' he exclaimed. 'Where are they? Don't say you left them behind!'

Gedanken looked at him scornfully. 'Why is it grown-ups never trust you to do anything properly?' She dangled them under his nose.

## 2 Wonky Space

'Guess what!' cried Gedanken, flinging open the back door and bursting into Uncle Albert's kitchen. 'I'm in a BAND!'

Uncle Albert was sitting at the table, with a cup of tea, head buried in the newspaper. 'A band?' he murmured, scarcely looking up. 'What sort of band?'

'A pop band, of course. A group.'

'How come? Don't you have to be able to play something?'

'I *can* play something. The keyboard. Got one for Christmas, remember?'

'Oh,' said Uncle Albert. 'That little piano thing . . .'

'Keyboards, I'll have you know, are much, much more difficult to play than pianos,' Gedanken exclaimed indignantly.

'Since when?' said Uncle Albert disbelievingly.

'You have to *programme* them, don't you? You have to put in all sorts of different sounds. You have to change the pitch – there's a pitch bender. You have to put in delays and reverbs. You have to know how to modulate, and sustain, and change the attack.'

Uncle Albert still looked unimpressed. 'Bit young to be playing in a band, aren't you? I'm surprised your parents let you.'

Gedanken looked a little uncomfortable. 'Well,' she said, 'I'm not exactly *in* the band – not yet.'

'What do you mean?'

'Well, I'm . . . attached to the band,' she mumbled. 'I rehearse with them. Sometimes. When it's OK with Dad.'

'Oh, I see.'

'Well, you've got to start somewhere. And when Jeremy's regular keyboard player left him to join another . . .'

'Jeremy! Not that hooligan we saw the other day – the one messing about in the dodgems.'

'Yes, if you must know,' said Gedanken defiantly. 'Jeremy's all right – when you get to know him. And he's a great musician – lead guitar. Everyone wants to get into his band. It's called The Stampede. And my friend Tracy's in it – she's on drums. Then there's Phil – bass guitar. He's really nice – much older than the rest of us. Mum and Dad think a lot of Phil. He told Dad he would see I was all right. It was because of Phil Dad said I could rehearse with them at weekends.'

Uncle Albert just quietly shook his head.

'Never mind, Uncle,' she said, patting him on the head, 'you're not into this, are you?'

They wandered slowly into the study and sat down.

'How was school today?' her uncle asked.

She shrugged. 'Friday. It's not so bad on a Friday. You get to do science. Which reminds me. Got anywhere with that gravity stuff?' she asked.

'Not really. I feel we're about to make some kind of breakthrough, but it's not there yet. I reckon we need to take a sideways step – see things from a different point of view. It might all fit together then – in a natural sort of way.'

'How do you mean?'

'Well, take my wheelbarrow, for instance. There it is sitting out on the garden path where I left it. If no one touches it, what will happen to it?'

'It'll just stay there, of course.'

'Right. There's no reason why it should do anything else. Staying put is the *natural* thing for it to do. It's natural for wheelbarrows; it's natural for anything else. It's only if something suddenly begins to move that you start asking questions. Why has it started moving in that particular direction? Why is it accelerating with that particular acceleration? It's then we start talking about forces.'

'Someone pushing the barrow?'

'Exactly. We say it goes in that direction because that is the direction he is pushing it. And it accelerates with that particular acceleration . . .'

'Because that's how hard he's pushing,' said Gedanken.

'Yes. That and what else?'

'How do you mean?' she asked.

'What else does the acceleration depend on? Does it matter if the barrow is empty or full?'

'Of course. Oh, I see. It depends on how heavy it is.'

'That's right. The amount of acceleration depends on how hard you push and how heavy the barrow is. OK. Now that's the normal way we think about things, and it makes a lot of sense. At least, it does if the force on the object is someone pushing a wheelbarrow. But when it comes to gravity . . . Well, for example, take those keys and the piece of paper. You let go of them on the Moon. You expected them to stay put. It's natural. If you had been out in the middle of space, far from anything else, they *would* have stayed put. But they didn't; they fell. So, we say there's a force – gravity. Now, you may say, "So what?" But the funny thing is they fell in *exactly* the same way. The keys fell to the ground just as fast as the paper, despite the keys being a lot heavier and needing more force. Now what I'm wondering is this: Instead of thinking that *staying put* is natural, and then having to introduce a force of gravity – which then mysteriously pulls on everything to make them all behave in exactly the same way – why not start out by saying that *falling* is the natural thing to do! Everything falling in exactly the same way is what is natural, *not* everything staying put the same way. If we make *that* our starting point, we can get rid of gravity forces altogether!'

'What *are* you on about?' asked Gedanken.

Ignoring her, Uncle Albert continued, 'And if an object is moving to begin with . . . Yes. Instead of thinking that it is natural for a moving object to carry on in a straight line at a steady speed, and then worrying about how the force of gravity manages to pull all objects – heavy ones and light ones – round in the same orbit, what we *ought* to be doing is thinking of the path they all follow as *being* the natural path. Yes. That must be it,' he said, getting more and more excited. 'For you and the Shuttle, near to the Earth, the natural path *wasn't* a straight line. It was the orbit you were both going in. The curved orbit was itself the natural path.'

'Uncle. I haven't a clue what you're on about. I'm still back with the wheelbarrow,' said Gedanken unhappily. 'You said the wheelbarrow was doing the natural thing – but it wasn't falling.'

'No it wasn't. The Earth was pushing up on it to stop it falling through the ground. So it *wasn't* in its natural state – not its natural falling state. We got that bit wrong.'

Gedanken felt more confused than ever. Uncle Albert noticed the look on her face and paused. A gleam came into his eye. 'Fancy another trip? Something different this time. Something we've never tried before. A visit to a different universe – one that might help you understand what I'm getting at?'

'A different *what*? A different *universe*! But how?' exclaimed Gedanken. 'There's only one universe – THE Universe. Isn't there?'

'Probably. No, what I've in mind is an *imaginary* universe.'

'You want Dick and me to . . .'

'No, no. Dick and the spacecraft are for exploring *this* universe. This time you'll have to go on your own.'

'On my own!? Not sure I like the sound of that.'

'Don't worry. You'll be all right – I think.'

'Well . . . If you say so,' said Gedanken nervously.

Already the thought-bubble had begun to appear above Uncle Albert's head. Gedanken studied it intently, but at first could see nothing. It seemed pitch black. But no. As her eyes got used to the darkness she began to see a tunnel – the interior of a tunnel. It stretched off into the distance. As she continued her searching look, trying to make out what might be at the far end, she became aware that she was gliding. Suddenly she realized that the bubble had disappeared and she was now gliding through the tunnel. She was on her way to – goodness knows where!

Eventually the tunnel widened. It was then she saw, directly ahead of her, a door. It marked the end of the tunnel. On it was written:

IMAGINARY UNIVERSES LABORATORY

She hesitated, not sure what to do next. There was nowhere else to go, so she knocked on the door. No reply. She gently pushed it, and immediately it swung open. She looked inside. No one about, so she went in. What a strange room! Set out on the benches were models of various shapes: a globe, a long horn, a ring-doughnut, and one that looked like a horse's saddle. On the floor was a pile of pebbles, in a corner a roll of rubber sheeting, in another a gleaming brass telescope. Maps were pinned to the walls. From the ceiling there hung a balloon, seemingly left over from a party. But her attention was drawn to a flashing sign mounted on a large metal box standing in the centre of the room:

CAUTION
TWO-DIMENSIONAL UNIVERSE
INVESTIGATION IN PROGRESS

Gedanken walked all round the box. It was completely closed up. Except that there was a microscope-like tube sticking out of one side. Filled with curiosity, she peered through it.

At first, she couldn't make it out. But then she realized that laid out before her was a flat surface. It extended as far as she could see in all directions. Directly below her were some tiny beetles crawling over the surface. They seemed very busy. Then came a larger beetle. He was dressed in a white coat – the sort that scientists wear. By his side was an assistant carrying a notepad and pencil. There was a flurry of excitement and hushed whispers of 'Shhh! Shhh! It's the professor!' The beetles stopped scurrying about.

'Are these the research students?' demanded the professor.

'Yes, sir,' said the assistant.

'Can't say they look particularly intelligent to me.'

'How rude,' thought Gedanken. 'I'm glad I don't have teachers like him.'

'Right,' he barked. 'Today we're doing geometry. Start by standing one behind the other to form a straight line. Stick out a front leg and touch the shoulder of the person in front of you.'

They dutifully did as they were told.

'Leg down. Left TURN!' he ordered. They turned, to face outwards from the line. 'On the order I want you all to march forward in straight lines. That way we shall investigate the behaviour of parallel lines.'

'Please sir,' came a shaky little voice.

'Who's that interrupting?' roared the professor.

'Mm . . mm . . me, sir,' came the timid reply. A small beetle had been pushed forward by the others.

'Well? What is it?'

'Pp . . pp . . please, sir. How do we know if we're going straight?'

'How . . . ?' The professor turned to the assistant. 'Is this really the best you can do?' Then, turning back to the offending beetle, he said slowly and deliberately, 'I take it you've got three legs on each side of your body. You have? Good. When you move forward, KEEP THEM LINED UP! Any more damned-fool questions? No? Then we'll get started. Ready. Steady. GO!'

With that, the line of beetles began their march forward like an army going into battle.

'Make a note of that,' the professor said to his assistant, sitting down at his desk and beginning to read a very fat, serious-looking book.

The assistant looked flustered. 'Excuse me, professor. A note of what, precisely?'

'Not *another* idiot!' fumed the professor. 'Heaven preserve me. A note of the fact that they have started out equally separated from each other, are now marching in parallel straight lines, and we need to check later that they are still separated by equal distances and still going in the same direction. Got it?'

'Yes, sir. Sorry sir,' mumbled the assistant.

'And don't hang about here! Get after them. Report back how things are going.'

'He really is disgustingly horrid, that professor,' thought Gedanken. 'If only I could get into this box, I'd squash him.'

At first all went well with the beetles. They strode confidently ahead in nice straight parallel lines. But then they got into trouble. The assistant rushed back to the professor. 'Sir. You had better come,' he said.

The professor hurried to the scene. He was furious. 'STOP!' he yelled. 'What on flat-Earth is going on? Can't I leave you for five minutes? I thought I told you to keep marching in straight lines.'

Again it was the turn of the timid one to speak up. 'P-please, sir, we *tried* to go in straight lines. Honestly, we did try ever so hard. It just seemed to go all wrong when we passed the big rock.'

'Rock! What rock?'

'The one back there, sir.'

What had happened was that, having marched in straight lines over open flat ground for a while, their paths had taken them close to a pebble. The pebble was resting in a hollow. As the beetles had marched past, those nearer the pebble had been deflected by the sloping surface – the closer to the pebble, the greater the change of direction.

The professor went to investigate. Sizing up the situation, he called in a loud voice, 'Gather round. I have an important announcement to make.'

Everyone respectfully obeyed, and tried to look interested.

31

'I have today discovered a new force. The rock exerts a force on beetles. As you marched past it, the force pulled you towards the rock. The closer you were to it, the stronger the force. Make a note of that. It's a very important fact.'

Gedanken could contain herself no longer.

'It's nothing of the sort,' she snorted. 'There's no force coming from that pebble. It's in a hollow. You changed direction because you followed the curve of the hollow.'

There was no response. None of the beetles seemed to have heard her. She repeated what she had said, only louder. Still no one heard. It was then Gedanken realized that all along she had been hearing the voices of the beetles over a loudspeaker. The sounds of what was going on in the box were being relayed out into the laboratory where Gedanken was, but nothing happening in the laboratory was getting through to the beetles in the box. It was very frustrating.

'But,' thought Gedanken, 'why isn't it *obvious* to them what's going on?' She studied the beetles closely. Then, for the first time she noticed how clumsy they were – they kept bumping into each other.

'Why, of course,' exclaimed Gedanken. 'That's it. They're blind! Well, almost. They can only see what's under their noses. They can't see far enough to make out the hollow.'

Sure enough. The beetles were short-sighted. This was why they hadn't caught on to the idea of the ground being curved, not flat – and so had to *invent* an imaginary force to explain what was going on.

'We must investigate the new force,' the professor declared.

'Yes, yes,' the beetles chanted in reply. 'The new force, the new force.'

With that they returned to the pebble. They marched past it, back and forth, marvelling at the way they were drawn towards it. Sure enough, the closer they approached, the greater was the change in direction, clearly showing that the force got stronger and stronger the closer you got to the pebble.

'Hey,' cried one of them. 'Look what's happening to me. I'm trying to go in a straight line but I keep ending up where I began. I must be going in a circle round the rock.'

Other beetles joined the first, and soon they were all crawling round the pebble in circles.

'Amazing,' exclaimed the professor to his assistant. 'Look at those there,' he said, pointing to two of the beetles. 'Different sizes, one heavier than the other, and yet they are going round exactly the same path in the same time. The force knows exactly how much harder it has to pull on the big one to keep it going in the same circle. How does it do it? *Why* does it do it? Another important fact. Make a note of it.'

'Important fact, my foot,' Gedanken exclaimed. 'It's got nothing to do with a force *at all*. They're going round the same circle because that is *the shape of the surface*. They're going round the sides of a hollow. They're on a racetrack – a banked racetrack. The surface isn't flat. It's WONKY!'

Just then the scene began to mist over. Soon she could no longer see anything clearly, nor could she make out what the beetles were saying.

The next thing she knew, she was back with Uncle Albert. Losing no time, she told him what had happened. '. . . and really, that so-called professor was so *thick*. It was unbelievable.'

'Shouldn't be too hard on him,' said Uncle Albert. 'It was all very well for you. You weren't short-sighted like him. Mind you, I agree. His measurements ought to have been enough to tell him his surface was curved – even if he couldn't *see* it. Why invent a mystery force that magically knows how hard to pull on everything to make them go round the same path when you could say that everything *has* to go in that curved path because that is how the space itself is curved? Much simpler. And you get rid of the idea of the force getting stronger the closer you get to the ball by saying the curvature gets greater.'

'Curvature? Gets *greater*? What exactly does . . .'

'The dome of St Paul's Cathedral is curved, right. So we say it has curvature. A tennis ball is more curved, so it has a greater curvature.'

'A pea?'

'Even more curvature.'

Gedanken thought for a moment. 'And a flat sheet of glass? No curvature at all?'

'Absolutely.'

'Oh, said Gedanken. 'You'd have thought those silly beetles would have got the idea. It's simple really.'

Uncle Albert began to chuckle.

'What's so funny?' asked Gedanken.

He looked at her closely. 'The beetles thought in terms of only two dimensions: forwards-and-backwards and leftwards-and-rightwards. They never caught on to the idea of the ground going upwards-and-downwards. For them it was flat, not curved. That was their mistake. Now the point I'm trying to make – the reason I sent you to that 2D universe – is that I reckon we're making the same mistake – about the space of *our* universe. I reckon our 3D space is curved!'

'*Our* space curved?! Couldn't be.'

'Why not?'

'There's nowhere for it to curve to.'

'Meaning?'

'Well, the beetles' surface starts off with only two dimensions. The up-and-down's not being used. You curve the surface by making it go *down* into a hollow. But with three-dimensional space there's no dimension left over. You can't hollow it, because there isn't anywhere for it to hollow into.'

'But that was what the professor beetle thought – about his surface. He couldn't see curvature in the third dimension. But we've just said that he should still have been able to *work out* that his space was curved, even though he couldn't *see* it. Perhaps our space is like that. It is wonky in a way that we can *work out*, even though we cannot see it curving off into any extra fourth dimension.'

'That's stupid. In any case, *why* say our space is curved?'

'Same reason as he should have said *his* was. We have invented a mystery force called gravity. It's just as fishy as his force. You and the Shuttle going round the Earth in the same orbit. Do you really think that was a coincidence – gravity pulling on the Shuttle harder like that so both of you end up doing exactly the same thing? That was what the professor thought about those two beetles going round the pebble. The *silly* professor,' he added with emphasis. 'He should have accepted that the two beetles were following the natural curve of the surface – it's simpler. In the same way, *we* in our turn should accept that you and the Shuttle were following the natural curve of *our* space.'

'But you're wrong! And I can prove it.'

'Oh? How?'

'Because space is *nothing*, and you can't curve nothing!' she declared triumphantly.

Uncle Albert thought for a moment. 'It's not made of matter – like the surface the beetles were on – but that's not to say it's nothing.'

'But it's empty. *Empty* space.'

'If there's no matter around, sure, we say it's "empty". But that only means it's empty of matter.

It doesn't mean that there's *nothing* left – neces-
sarily. We might be left with a thin, transparent,
invisible, jelly-like space.'

'You're joking.'

'No. I'm perfectly serious. A jelly might sometimes have lumps of fruit in it, just as space can have
lumps of matter in it – the Earth, the Sun, the Moon.
Take the fruit away, and you still have the jelly.'

'You're saying space is like a wobbly jelly?'

Uncle Albert smiled. 'That's not a very scientific
way of talking. But, yes. It's a bit like that. If you put
a lump of matter into space, it distorts and curves
the space around it. Matter tells space how to curve;
then the curvy space tells matter how to move
through it.'

Gedanken still did not look at all happy.

'A problem?' asked Uncle Albert.

She shrugged. 'What you're saying *seems* to make
sense. But somehow . . . invisible distorting jellies
. . . It's all a bit . . . oh, I don't know . . .'

'You'd like a mental picture of what's going on.'

'Yes,' she said, brightening up. 'That's what I
want. I want a picture. I want to *see* what's going
on.'

'Well, you can't. And that's all there is to it. It's
like that in science sometimes – really deep science –
what we call "physics". Sometimes you can't form a
picture of what's going on. You just have to allow
the arguments to guide you. It's a bit like those
planes that land in the fog at night. The pilot would
*like* to see what's ahead but can't. He has to rely on

37

his instruments. But he still lands all right.'

Gedanken looked across at the clock. 'I've got to go. There's a rehearsal tomorrow, and I've got some history homework to do before.' She got up to leave, but then stopped. 'Tell me, Uncle, is it all right to carry on thinking about ordinary gravity force instead of wonky space – if you want to?'

'Depends. Depends on whether they come up with the same results. If they both say the world behaves in exactly the same way, you can't say one is right and the other wrong. It's only if they come up with different . . .'

Uncle Albert paused. He looked very thoughtful. 'I wonder . . .' he murmured.

'What's up?' asked Gedanken.

'Of course. Should have thought of it before. Sorry, Gedanken. I need you to go back to that two-dimensional universe again. Just for a moment. Do you mind?'

'But, I'm late already . . .' she protested.

'*Please*.'

'It's all right for you. What's Mum going to say?'

'I'll give her a ring,' said Uncle Albert. 'I'll tell her it was my fault.'


Finding herself back in the Imaginary Universes Laboratory, Gedanken lost no time in looking down the microscope again. The beetles were now standing around in pairs, each pair holding a length of string, a piece of chalk, and a tape measure.

'Right, you lot,' shouted the professor. 'We're

now going to investigate the properties of circles. One of you stands still holding one end of the string; the other walks round marking out a circle with the chalk on the ground, holding the other end and keeping the string pulled tight. Each string has a different length so you will each be investigating a different size circle. Next, with the tape, I want you to measure the distance round the circle – that's called the CIRCUMFERENCE. Then, lay the tape *across* the circle, from one side to the other, passing the person in the centre, and measure that too; that's the DIAMETER. You then find their ratio. Is that clear?'

There was an embarrassed silence. Then a familiar timid voice spoke up: 'Ratio, sir?'

'Yes, RATIO! You divide the circumference by the diameter. You find out how many diameters make a circumference! Good grief, have you no brains at all? Look, if you can't do sharing sums, give your readings to my assistant. He'll work them out for you on his calculator. You *have* got your calculator with you, haven't you?' he said, glaring savagely over his shoulder at the assistant.

'Er. Yes, sir,' replied the assistant.

'Right! Get to it!'

The beetles immediately started running around in circles chalking the ground, and falling over themselves as they stretched the tape measure across from one side of the circle to the other. On finishing their measurements, they scurried over to the assistant who then worked out the ratios for them. As he did so, his eyes began to widen in astonishment.

'Sir, sir,' he said.

'What is it?' asked the professor.

'An important fact. The circumference is three times the diameter. It doesn't matter how big or small the circle, the ratio is always three!'

'*Exactly* three?'

'Er. Not quite. A bit more. It's more like 3.142. But it is *always* 3.142.'

'3.142, eh? Funny sort of number. Make a note of it.'

'Yes sir.'

Just then the last pair turned up with their measurements. The assistant again busied himself with his calculator.

'Oh . . .' he exclaimed. He repeated the calculation. 'Are you sure you haven't made a mistake?' he whispered to the pair. They looked at each other, and shook their heads. The assistant began banging his calculator on the ground and holding it up to his ear.

'Whatever is the matter?' asked the professor.

'Not working properly.'

'Why? What's wrong with it?'

'Keeps giving the wrong answer. Should be 3.142, but now it's smaller. I reckon the battery is running down . . .'

'WHAT? Smaller numbers, so the battery must be . . .! Here, give it to me. What were the readings?' He snatched the calculator and repeated the sum.

'Good Heavens! You're right.'

'The battery is . . .'

'No, not *that*! The ratio of the circumference to the diameter. It *is* smaller.' He demanded to know where this odd circle was. The beetles led the way to where they had done their measurements. 'This is it, sir,' said one of them, pointing to the circle they had drawn on the ground.

'Hmmm,' said the professor, exploring it. 'Seems a perfectly good circle to me. Nice straight diameter. But what's this? This here in the middle? A rock? Was this here when you did your measurements?'

'Er, yes, sir,' said one of the beetles. 'Sorry, sir. But I was tired. All that marching we did earlier. I only had to hold the end of the string, while my friend went round the circle, so I thought I'd have a rest, and so . . . I found this . . . and sat on it. That's why it's in the middle of the circle.'

Gedanken giggled. She guessed what had gone wrong. The pebble, like the earlier one they had come across, was resting in a hollow. The circle these beetles had drawn was where the ground was wonky.

The professor thought for a moment, then said to his assistant, 'A tape measure. Get me a 1-metre tape measure.' The assistant found him one. He then proceeded to draw a circle of diameter 1 metre on a flat piece of ground. He then laid the tape across the diameter so that it exactly stretched from one side of the circle to the other.

'Right,' he said. 'That is a normal circle. The circumference is 3.142 metres, the diameter 1 metre. Now I want you to place that rock of yours in the centre of my circle.'

With much huffing and puffing, the beetles managed to lift the pebble and carry it over to the professor's circle. There they gently laid it down on top of the 50-centimetre mark at the middle of the tape measure. Immediately there was a flurry of excitement.

'Look, look!' exclaimed the assistant. 'The tape measure no longer stretches across the circle.'

Sure enough, it didn't. As the heavy stone had been placed in the middle of the circle, the ground had given way a little. It seemed to be made of rubber. The tape measure had now to go down into the hollow as well as across the circle, and it was not long enough to do this. Gedanken suddenly remembered the roll of rubber sheeting – the one she had seen in the corner of the laboratory. She glanced across at it. 'Of course. That's why the pebbles always end up making dents.'

'Gather round!' the professor beamed. 'Another important discovery. You all saw that to begin with the tape measure stretched across from one side to the other, exactly. Now it doesn't. Why? Because the force of the rock has *shrunk* the tape measure.'

'Wonderful!' cried the beetles. 'Hooray for the professor. He has done it again.'

Gedanken lost her patience.

'Stupid!' she exclaimed. 'It did nothing of the sort. The tape measure is perfectly all right. It's the ground that's been stretched. Why *can't* you work it out properly?'

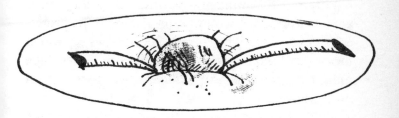

But it was no good. She found herself back with Uncle Albert.

'Brilliant!' he declared excitedly as she finished telling him what had happened. He punched the air like a footballer scoring a goal. 'I thought so. It must be the same with *our* world too.'

'What's the same?' asked Gedanken.

'What you found out: Things shrinking when they get close to heavy objects. Gravity shrinks them.'

'Gravity *what*?' Gedanken exploded in disbelief. 'In *our* space – our three-dimensional space . . .?'

'Yes. Must be. Can't imagine why no one's thought of it before.'

'But the beetles' tape measure *didn't* shrink. Not *really*. It just appeared that way because they couldn't see the wonkyness of the rubber,' said Gedanken.

'Fair enough. *You* were looking at the beetle world in such a way as to be able to see the third dimension. For you the tape measure didn't shrink – it just followed the wonkyness of the two-dimensional surface as it hollowed out into the third dimension. But for a beetle who can think only in terms of two dimensions, it *does* appear to shrink. The important thing is that circles near heavy objects are different from normal. The ratio of the circumference to the diameter is less. Why? Because the distance across the diameter has got longer – according to you. Either that, or the tape being used to measure the distance shrinks – according to the beetles. It shrinks when it lies *across* the circle – along a diameter – compared to what it's like when measuring *round* the circle. Distances getting longer, tape measures getting shorter – either way, it comes to the same thing.'

'And you're saying that our space is like that too?'

'Yes. Must be. The circle the Shuttle makes as it orbits the Earth must be one of those funny circles.'

'Because the Earth is making the space wonky.'

'Exactly. If you were to measure the diameter of the Shuttle's orbit it would be longer than it would be if the Earth weren't there.'

'If the Earth weren't there, the Shuttle wouldn't be in orbit. Hah! Got you there!'

Uncle Albert laughed. 'You know what I mean, clever dick.'

Gedanken thought for a moment. 'You said the diameter would be longer. Would it *look* longer?'

'You wouldn't see it curving off into another dimension, or anything like that; it would still look perfectly straight. But we could tell that it was longer because of the extra tape measures it would take to get from one side to the other.'

'But that could be because the tape measures have shrunk, you said?'

'Yes, that's the other way of looking at it.'

'And the shrinking gets more the closer in you get?'

'That's right.'

'And the shrinking affects everything – not just tape measures?'

'Of course. They all shrink in the direction of the diameter of the circle – the vertical direction if you're standing on the Earth. So,' he continued, 'if you had a tall skyscraper, say, with people living at the top, they will think everything at the bottom has shrunk – been squashed down – compared to normal.'

'Won't that seem odd – to the people living on the ground floor – to have everything around them squashed up?'

'Ah, but it won't seem squashed to *them*. *Everything* is smaller down there – including their eyeballs – to the same extent – so the eye still gets filled up with what it's looking at in the normal way. And, of course, you can't *measure* anything to show that it's shorter than usual . . .'

'Because the tape measure also shrinks?'

'Exactly. By the same amount. So life at the bottom carries on normally, and everything around you looks normal. It's only when you are on the top floor and you look down on life on the bottom floor that everything down there looks smaller than normal.'

'And what if you live on the ground floor and you look up at what's going on at the top? What will that look like?'

'Questions, questions! Work it out for yourself.'

Gedanken thought for a moment. 'If you live on the ground floor your eyeball is squashed. But you're looking at things on the top floor where they're not squashed – not to the same extent at any rate – so . . . they would look . . . *bigger* than normal . . . yes?'

'That's right. It's not difficult.'

A gleam came into Gedanken's eye. 'Hey. If that's true, I'm going to make a bomb out of this,' she announced. 'I'm going to get really, really rich.'

'Oh. And how do you intend doing that?'

'I'll look for a department store that sells dress material on the top floor. I'll get the assistant to measure it out holding the material and the tape measure vertically, and I'll buy lots and lots. And then I'll sell it to another store that sells it on the ground floor.'

'That's supposed to make your fortune?'

'Yep. It's all figured out. I'm buying material where the tape measures are big, so I get extra, and I sell it where the tape measures are small, so they don't get as much as they think they've got. Pretty smart, eh?'

Uncle Albert sighed. 'These get-rich-quick

schemes of yours. In the first place the shrinking produced by the Earth is too small to notice. Its gravity is too weak. In the second, what do you think happens to the material as you carry it downstairs?'

'What do you mean?'

'Think, Gedanken. Think,' said Uncle Albert wearily.

Gedanken's face fell. 'Oh, I see. It shrinks.'

'Exactly.'

As she walked home in the dark, she thought to herself, 'Why is there always a catch to it? There's nothing for it. I'll *have* to get a regular place in the group. Then when The Stampede cuts its first disc . . .!'

A thought suddenly hit her. 'O Lor! I should have reminded him to ring Mum.'

## 3  The Big Bang

'Tell me something interesting, Uncle.' Gedanken lazily trailed her hand in the water. The river bank slid by as their boat was gently carried along. A church bell was ringing in the distance.

'Something interesting?' replied Uncle Albert. He pulled the oars aboard. It was hot, and he was glad of the rest. He thought for a moment. 'How about: You are made of stardust!'

'What does that mean?' asked Gedanken.

'Do you know what stars are?'

'Tiny planets?' she suggested.

'Not exactly. Planets are cold, mostly rocky – like the Earth. A star is like the Sun – a ball of fire – hot fiery gas.'

'But very, very tiny,' said Gedanken.

'Not at all. They're as big as the Sun – some are even bigger.'

She frowned.

'That church over there,' he said, pointing. 'Looks tiny, right? Is it really that small?'

''Course not. It's a long way off.'

'Exactly. If you were close up, it would look nor-mal. Distance makes things look small. Same with stars. They're actually huge. The Sun *is* a star – *our* star.'

'Wouldn't call *that* huge,' said Gedanken trying to squint up at the Sun.

'A hundred times the diameter of the Earth, and you don't call that huge?'

'Is it really that big?' asked Gedanken.

'Yes. That too is a long way off, but nothing like as far as the stars.'

'But,' she continued hesitantly, 'what about the points?'

'What points?'

'The ones on stars. You get them on drawings . . .'

'*Those*,' laughed Uncle Albert. 'That's just a trick of the eyesight. Like car headlights. When a car comes towards you in the dark, its lights seem to have spikes on. You must have noticed. But only when it's far off. As soon as it gets close, they don't – they look round and ordinary.'

'So stars are just big round balls of fire?'

'That's right.'

'How many are there?'

'Lots. Too many to count. They're gathered together in groups called "galaxies". Each galaxy can have . . . ooh . . . 100,000 million stars.'

Gedanken was impressed. 'Is our Sun in a galaxy?'

'Yes. We call it the Galaxy – with a capital G. Mind you, as galaxies go, it's nothing special – just one of 100,000 million galaxies. There are the same number of galaxies as there are stars in any one galaxy. And even the Sun itself is nothing special either. To someone on a planet a long, long way off it would look just like an ordinary star.'

'And do all the stars have gravity?'

'Of course.'

Gedanken thought for a minute, then said, 'In that case, they should all land up in the middle – of their galaxy. Because they're all pulling on each other.'

'Like the Moon lands up on the surface of the Earth?' asked Uncle Albert.

'What do you mean? The Moon doesn't land up . . .'

'Of course it doesn't. But the Earth's gravity is still pulling on it – trying to pull it closer.'

'But that's different. That's because it's going round in a circle – like the Shuttle, and me on my space walk. We've been through all that.'

'Yes, and it's the same reason why the stars don't clump together in the middle of the galaxy. They're going round and round.'

'Round and round what?' persisted Gedanken.

'Round and round the centre of the galaxy.'

'Oh.' She thought for a moment, then added, 'And what about the galaxies themselves? You said there were lots of galaxies, right? Well, do the different galaxies go round each other?'

'No.'

'Then what keeps *them* from clumping together – in the middle of the Universe?'

He didn't answer. He just stared at the water.

'Well?' inquired Gedanken impatiently.

'Don't know. You're right; they *ought* to pull themselves together at one place. But they don't. Hadn't thought of that . . .'

Gedanken didn't see what this had to do with her being made of stardust – or whatever it was her uncle had said. In any case, she had now got to thinking of other things. Yesterday's rehearsal – if you could call it that. What a shambles! The problem was they didn't have a proper place to rehearse. 'Can't have it here. Too much noise.' The number of times they'd heard that. Then there were difficulties over transport. They really needed a van to take all their gear. Eventually Phil's dad had let them borrow his garage. But then too late they realized there was only the one power point in the garage and they hadn't got enough adaptors to take all the amplifiers and instruments.

They were now drifting down river much faster than before. Gedanken looked about her.

'What's a weir, Uncle?' she asked.

'A what?'

'W-E-I-R,' she said, spelling it out. 'On that notice up there on the bank.'

'Where? What does it say? Haven't got my glasses.'

She read it out:


DANGER
WEIR AHEAD
NO BOATS BEYOND THIS POINT

'What?! Why didn't you tell me?'

'I did. Just then,' she replied indignantly.

Uncle Albert picked up the oars, turned the boat round, and started furiously rowing up river. It was hard work. Uncle Albert was soon puffing and blowing. But the further they got from the area, the easier it became. Once out of danger he relaxed. 'Phew. That could have been nasty. Not as strong as I used to be.'

'What *was* that all about?' asked Gedanken.

'A weir – a kind of waterfall. You get them on rivers. As you get close, the water flows faster and faster. Too close and you get swept over the edge – except that they usually have some sort of wire-mesh barrier to stop you at the last moment. That's why boats have to keep their distance.' Then he added sheepishly, 'Sorry I shouted. My fault. Should have spotted it myself.'

Gedanken smiled, 'I won't let on,' adding as an afterthought, 'at least, not if you do me a favour.'

'Oh,' he said suspiciously. 'What might that be?'

'A quick ride in the spacecraft when we get back?'

'Heh! How many treats do you want in one day?'

'Oh go on, Uncle. It might help in our research.'

Uncle Albert laughed. 'And *what* exactly do you have in mind?' he asked.

'Well . . .' she began, trying to think of something, 'I could . . . I could go and investigate the galaxies for you. How about that? I could see what stops them falling in on top of each other.'

'Some hopes. Still, it would do no harm for you to

see what a galaxy looks like. And we have to get this boat back by one o'clock anyway. And I don't like the look of those clouds coming up. Wouldn't surprise me if we've had the best of the day. OK,' he decided, 'Once we get home, a bite of lunch, and I'll beam you up for a quick one.'

'Hi, Dick!' Gedanken called out cheerily as she arrived in the spacecraft.

'Good afternoon, Captain,' replied the computer. 'Sudden change of plan or something? I wasn't expecting you today.'

'Yes. Sort of,' she said, looking out of the window. 'Where are we? Can't see much.'

'We're just outside the Galaxy. I'll swing the craft round so you can get a better look at it.'

There was a throb of rocket motors, and the craft rotated. As it did, the Galaxy came into view. Gedanken had never seen such an awesome sight. Laid out before her was a gigantic swirl of stars. They were arranged in the form of a great flattened disc. As she watched she could see that the disc was slowly rotating – rather like a record on a turntable.

'What do you think of *that*?' asked Dick.

'Brilliant!' exclaimed Gedanken. 'Where's the Sun?'

'Can't really see it from here. Just a tiny speck about two-thirds of the way out from the centre.'

'Where are the other galaxies? Uncle said there were more.'

'Yes. Lots of them. But they're all a long way off,

and they look very faint. Hang on a minute. I'll swing the craft back round again so you don't get blinded by the glare from our galaxy. There.'

Gedanken had to wait a minute for her eyes to get used to the inky black darkness again. But then she made out a very tiny-looking patch of light in the distance – then another, and another. In fact the sky was full of them. 'Is that them?' asked Gedanken. 'Those smudges?'

'That's right. Each of those smudges, as you call

them, is a galaxy like ours.'

'Can I go and visit one of them?'

'Well, I don't know about that . . .'

'*Please*. I'm supposed to investigate them to find out why they don't all fall together.'

'But they do seem to be a long way off. I'm not sure we have time . . .'

'Just one . . . or two?'

'Oh well. I'll check the records and see. There might be one close enough.'

There was a pause. Then Dick said, 'First one's no good. Too far and it's going away from us . . . Next one, even further, and going away even faster . . . And the next, same again, going away . . . And the next, too far, and going away . . . And the . . .'

'Dick,' interrupted Gedanken, 'Did you say they were going *away* from us?'

'Yes.'

'*All* of them?'

'Seems so.'

'Give me a list, will you?'

Up on the monitor screen came a list of the galaxies, their distance from the Galaxy and how fast they were moving. Gedanken studied this intently. Sure enough, all the galaxies were moving away from our galaxy. Moreover, she noted that the further away they were, the faster they were going. Twice as far away, twice the speed; three times the distance, three times the speed; ten times the distance, ten times the speed, and so on. 'How very peculiar,' she thought.

On returning to the study, she told Uncle Albert of her discovery.

'But that's extraordinary!' he declared, hardly able to contain himself. 'You've solved the problem!'

'What problem?' said Gedanken. 'What I want to know is what's wrong with us and our galaxy? Why is everyone trying to get away from us?'

'The problem of why the galaxies don't all pile in on top of each other. Some time in the past there must have been an almighty explosion. A great BANG, and all the matter of the Universe – all the stuff – must have come hurtling out. And it's still all flying apart.'

'You're making this up.'

'No, I'm not. It's what you told me. You said the further away the galaxy was, the faster it was going. Twice the distance, twice the speed, right?'

'Yes. So?'

'Well, that's exactly what you'd get if there'd been a big explosion with everything starting out from the same place. If you go twice as fast as something else, and you started out at the same instant from the same spot, you'd go twice as far – which is what you found. Gravity tries to pull things together again, but the violence of the explosion – the fact that they start off moving outwards in all directions – keeps them apart. For a time, anyway.'

'What do you mean – "for a time"?'

'Well, gravity's pulling on them – slowing them down. One day they might slow right down and start to fall back again – like a stone thrown into the air – it slows down, pauses for a moment, and then falls back again. On the other hand, they might be moving too fast for gravity to bring them back – like a rocket leaving the pull of Earth's gravity.'

'And when's this all supposed to have happened – this explosion?'

'Well, judging from where the galaxies are today, it must have happened ages ago – thousands of millions of years ago. It would take that long for them to get so far apart.'

He sat back in his armchair with a look of supreme satisfaction. 'To think – the Universe was created in a Big Bang.'

'Thought God was supposed to have created everything.'

'Possibly. But *how* did he do it? That's what we're asking.'

'And you're saying it began with a Big Bang?'

'Right.'

'So, what blew up? A planet?'

'No. There wouldn't have been any planets or stars then. Everything was too violent and hot. It must have spewed out as a gas – a blindingly hot gas.'

'So where do the planets come from?'

'Well, first the gas has to cool down and collect into whirlpools – the galaxies. The galaxies then develop smaller whirlpools – hot balls of gas that become stars . . .'

'And planets.'

'No . . .' said Uncle Albert thoughtfully. 'Not at

this stage. Up to now all we've got are light gases – the gases that came out of the Big Bang. No rocky material. The Big Bang was *violent* – so violent that only the smallest bits of atomic particles could have survived. Anything bigger would have got smashed up. And that means you start off with the atomic bits that make up the lightest gases – the sort you get in stars. So, at first all you get are stars.'

'But what about the rocks and stuff?' demanded Gedanken.

'Will you be PATIENT! I'm getting there as fast as I can. The heavier atomic bits – the stuff that goes to make up the planets – they had to wait until later – until they'd had a chance to be built up. That was done *inside the stars*. It's very hot in there. So hot that some of the small atomic bits of gas stick together to form the bigger bits needed later for making rocks.'

'Like sweets,' interrupted Gedanken.

'Eh?' asked Uncle Albert.

'Like sweets. When it's a hot day they melt and stick together and you can pretend you can't get them apart. You can eat two or three all in one go then.'

Uncle Albert smiled. 'Sort of. We call it *nuclear fusion*. Anyway,' he continued, 'after the fusion, some of the stars explode.'

'Explode?'

Uncle Albert nodded.

'Why?'

'Oh Lor, this is getting very complicated,' said Uncle Albert. He searched around for a way of explaining it. 'Well, let's put it this way. It all happens when the star gets very, very old . . .'

'Oh, I see,' said Gedanken. 'Why didn't you say?'

Uncle Albert looked at her in surprise. 'What do you mean?' he asked. 'You *understand* why the star blows up?'

'Yes. Of course. You said it got old.'

'So?'

'It got silly,' said Gedanken. 'What next?'

Uncle Albert looked a bit put out, but decided to let it pass. 'Well,' he continued, 'the materials thrown out of the exploding star went to form further stars – like our Sun, and the planets – like the Earth. And some was used to make people.'

'People?!' Gedanken looked down at herself, and at her hands. 'You mean all this came out of exploding *stars!*'

'That's right – the raw materials. You're made of stardust. That's what I told you in the boat.'

Gedanken could hardly believe it. 'Wow. That's brilliant!' she breathed. 'Hey, I can't wait to tell them at school. Made of stardust, and sitting at the centre of the Universe.'

'Hold on. Who said anything about "sitting at the centre of the Universe"?' asked Uncle Albert.

'I did. It's obvious. The Big Bang happened here – right where we are. Everything moves away from *us*. Right? That's what I found out.'

Uncle Albert frowned. He slowly shook his head. 'I see what you mean. But no way can that be right.'

'Why not? Don't you like being special? I do.'

'Gedanken, our galaxy is an ordinary galaxy. A very ordinary galaxy. There is no reason why, out of the whole Universe, it should be us at the centre.'

'*Someone's* got to be at the centre. So why not us? After all, everyone else *is* going away from us.'

'I know, I know that. But it's all too much of a fluke. We just *aren't* that special. There must be some other reason . . . I wonder . . . I just . . .'

With that, the thought-bubble began to appear above his head.

'Wonder what, Uncle?' asked Gedanken, her curiosity aroused.

'Fancy another ride?' he asked.

Gedanken nodded.

On arriving at the Imaginary Universes Laboratory, Gedanken immediately took a look into the experimental box. This time she saw pebbles laid out over the whole of the surface, more or less evenly spaced. Each rested in a hollow. She wondered why they didn't all run together in the middle. But then she noticed a peculiar thing. Instead of coming together, they were actually moving apart! She was directly over one of the pebbles and could see that all the others were moving away from hers. And, yes, the further away the other pebbles, the faster they retreated into the distance. 'How odd,' she thought. 'The pebbles are behaving just like the galaxies. I'm at the centre of this universe as well.'

Just then she heard a familiar voice.

'Right, you blithering idiots. Time's up.' It was

the professor beetle. He was standing next to her pebble, yelling through a megaphone at the other beetles who were scattered all over the sheet measuring up circles drawn round all the various pebbles. 'Stop what you're doing. Back to base!'

The beetles dutifully gathered up their tape measures, string and chalk, and began to return. Those with least distance to travel arrived first, as one would expect. Then came those from further away. Except, Gedanken noticed, those who had to travel quite a long way. These were walking just as fast as the others – yet, for some reason, they hardly seemed to get any closer to the professor!

How very strange. Gedanken thought there must be something wrong with her eyesight – the strain of looking down the microscope. Perhaps she ought to take a break. She looked about her. Again her attention was drawn to the roll of rubber sheeting. She wandered across the laboratory to where it was propped up against the wall. She felt it and discovered that it was very soft and stretchy. As she did so, a thought struck her. Stretchy! Of course! Why hadn't it occurred to her before? She hurried back to the microscope. Yes, that was it! It was obvious. The rubber sheet – the one the beetles were walking on – was stretching. It was *expanding in all directions*.The expansion of the surface was what was causing the pebbles to move away from hers – they were being carried along by the movement of the sheet. And it was this same movement that was now making it difficult for the distant beetles to get back to the professor. It was a bit like the rowing boat trying to make headway against the flow of the river near the weir.

Uncle Albert was thrilled to hear Gedanken's description of what had happened. 'Terrific! Explains everything. Explains why the galaxies in *our* universe are moving apart – not falling together. *Our* space must be expanding – just like the rubber sheet. The expanding space is carrying the galaxies along with it. And those beetles of yours – the ones that couldn't get home because the sheet was moving almost as fast as they could walk – that must be how it is for light moving through our space. Light given out by distant galaxies has to swim against the tide of expansion to get to us. And if it's coming from the farthest reaches of space – where the tide of expansion flows really fast – it will still not have reached us – even though it started out on its journey at the beginning of the Universe, thousands of millions of years ago.'

'But I still don't see why we're at the centre of the Universe,' said Gedanken. 'There's nothing special about our galaxy, you said. And there wasn't anything special about my pebble. So why does it all move away from us? Why not from somewhere else?'

'But it does.'

'Does what?'

'Move away from somewhere else. It moves away from everywhere else. It's *space itself* that is expanding. The space between *all* pairs of galaxies gets bigger, so *all* galaxies get further away from each other. It doesn't matter which galaxy you're on. From *any* chosen viewpoint it looks as though every other galaxy is going away from you. Look!' He pulled out a pen and drew five dots in a line along the edge of his newspaper. 'Five galaxies, right? Separated by equal distances.' Then, drawing another five dots with a wider spacing between them, he added, 'The same five galaxies sometime later. The space between each one has expanded, yes?'

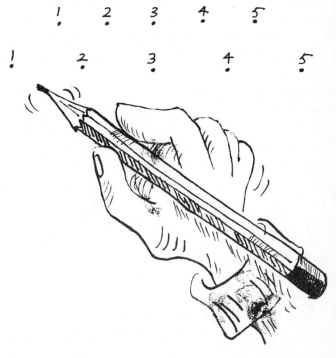

Gedanken nodded.

'As far as the galaxy in the middle here is concerned, the others have moved away from it. But the same is true for galaxy number two; the others have moved away from *it*. And galaxy number one, and four, and five. It's the same for all of them.'

'Oh, I get it,' said Gedanken brightening. 'Yes, obvious, really. So they *all* think they're at the centre of the Big Bang.'

'That's right. But really there is no centre. It isn't that all the matter in the Universe started off from one particular point in space and then kept on expanding into the rest of the space. The Big Bang doesn't happen *in* space at all. It marks the moment when space itself was created.'

'Does that mean it's still being created? It's getting bigger, right. So there's more space today than there was yesterday . . .'

'Exactly.'

'So it's like a jelly that's always getting bigger – you said space was like a jelly – an invisible one, remember? Wow! I wish real jellies were like that,' said Gedanken. 'What a way to make money!'

Uncle Albert laughed. 'That reminds me: it's teatime. And guess what's on the menu.'

'Really?'

Uncle Albert nodded. 'Not the expanding sort, but I reckon it'll be big enough.'

# 4 The Circular Tour – in a Straight Line

'Never knew you played the violin, Uncle,' said Gedanken, entering the study. 'Thought the noise was coming from the radio.'

'Been playing since I was a boy. Surprised you didn't know.'

She took off her jacket and slung it down on the settee. 'Do you just play on your own?'

'Mostly. Sometimes with friends.'

Gedanken started to giggle. 'In a band?'

'Wouldn't exactly call it a *band*,' said Uncle Albert. 'More a string trio.'

She hadn't heard of one of those.

'Get to do any gigs?' she asked.

He smiled and shook his head.

'*We've* got one coming up. New Bands Night at the youth club.'

'The youth club? What goes on there?'

'Nothing much. Mostly we just hang about.'

'Sounds a waste of time to me.'

'Well it's not,' said Gedanken indignantly. 'You're with friends, and that's what matters. I can't help it if you're stand-offish,' she blurted out.

Uncle Albert looked at her sharply, then turned

away. She knew she shouldn't have said that. 'Sorry,' she mumbled. 'Didn't mean . . .'

'Oh it's all right. Nothing to be sorry about. I know what they say about me. And they're right – up to a point. I do like my own company. I need space – so I can think.'

Gedanken came and sat on the floor close to his chair. 'I know how you feel, sort of,' she said. 'Dad's always telling me off about watching too much TV. I'm too shut off, he says. Becoming a zombie. Ought to be out playing all the time. But it's not like that. When I'm watching TV, I'm thinking. I'm learning about myself.'

They sat in silence for a while. Then Gedanken said, 'Uncle, if you like being on your own a lot, why do you put up with me? You do like it when I visit you, don't you?'

Uncle Albert smiled reassuringly. 'You're different.'

'How?'

'Because you don't stop me thinking. You actually *help* me – by the questions you ask.'

'That reminds me. I wanted to ask you something – about gravity. You know how you said we ought to stop thinking about gravity forces – between the Earth and the Shuttle – and we ought to think of curvature instead – the Shuttle following the curve of space.'

'Yes.'

'Well, when we were going on about the Universe and all the galaxies and the Big Bang, we talked about gravity forces – between the galaxies – trying to pull them together. We didn't talk about curvature then. So when we talk of *galaxies*, do we *have* to think of forces, and not curved space?'

She waited for a reply. When none came she turned and looked up at him. There above his head, shining brightly, was the thought-bubble.

'Why don't you go and investigate,' he suggested.

'How? I've already been out among the galaxies.'

'Perhaps the professor beetle can help,' said Uncle Albert with a twinkle in his eye.

Down in the experimental box all was excitement. The beetles were crowded together shouting, waving flags, and holding banners. Gedanken peered closely and saw that one of the banners said 'Good luck!', another 'Come back soon!', and another 'Hooray for the Daring Explorer!' All attention was fixed on a car shaped like a bullet. In it sat a tiny beetle wearing goggles. He was receiving last-minute instructions from the professor.

'Have you got everything? Food. Drink.'

The driver nodded. To Gedanken, the poor little thing looked very, very nervous. She thought it might be the one that was always being made to speak up for the others, but she couldn't be sure; it's difficult to tell one beetle from another.

'Right, you know what you have to do. See the arrow I've painted on the ground? That is the direction you have to go. You go straight forward in a dead straight line. You never change direction. Just keep going and going, until you eventually come to the edge of the universe. You won't be able to miss it. That's where the road ends – where the ground stops. Right? You note how far you've gone. That way we'll know how big the universe is. You take a look round to see what is outside our universe. Then turn the car round, and come straight back. It's a very fast car, so it shouldn't take too long. You have a full tank of petrol and some reserve supplies at the back. Good luck.'

Turning to the crowd, the professor shouted. 'Out of the way, you idiots! Do you want to get run down?'

The crowd hastily cleared a corridor for the car.

'Right, off you go!' he yelled.

'Ye-es, s-sir,' came the timid reply. The engine started up and the car edged forward. Shouts and cheers all round. The car picked up speed and shot off into the distance. Soon it could no longer be seen by the naked eye, but the professor continued to watch it through binoculars. 'Excellent, excellent,' he murmured. 'Straight as a die.' After a further period, even he could no longer see it.

Everyone quietly settled down for a long wait. Some had brought folding chairs. These were set out facing the way the explorer had gone so as to ensure a good view of him on his return. Others sat on the ground. Some began to eat their sandwiches; others lit barbeques. A few tents were erected.

'Of course,' said one beetle knowingly, 'we shall never see him again. It's well known that the universe is infinite. It has no end. Our friend will carry on for ever and never return.'

'Surely not,' said another. 'The professor wouldn't send anyone to their death like that.' The first one looked at him as if to say 'Are you kidding?'

Another joined in. 'Can't imagine infinity. It's a daft idea. Mind you, I don't think we'll see him again. I reckon he'll get to the end of the universe and that'll be that. He'll go drifting off the edge into another universe and will never be able to get back.'

So the guessing game continued. The beetle children got bored with peering into the distance. They began annoying their parents by constantly asking when the car would be back so they could go home and watch television. They were told to go off and play.

Then all of a sudden, a beetle squealed, 'Quiet, everybody! I can hear something.'

A hush descended. Sure enough, in the distance could be heard the sound of the car returning. Great excitement. Everyone started shouting and cheering again. They eagerly scanned the horizon where they had last seen the car disappear. The roar of the engine got louder and louder. But still they could see no sign of it. 'Where is it? Where is it?' they cried. The sound became deafening; it must be right up to them – but *still* no sign.

Then, a loud screech of brakes. It came from *behind* them. Yes, that's right: from directly *behind* them. Everyone spun round. There was the car. Total confusion. The driver got out grinning sheepishly – but not for long. Striding towards him was the professor. He was in a towering rage.

'How dare you disobey orders!' he barked. 'I told you to keep going in the same direction. *That* one!' he yelled, pointing the way the car had originally disappeared. 'The direction of the painted arrow.'

'But, s-sir. I *did* keep going in that direction. I'm *still* pointing in that direction.' And of course, he was right: the car was accurately lined up with the arrow.

For a moment, the professor looked flustered. But then he pulled himself together. 'Don't play games with me, my boy,' he said. 'When you got to the edge of the universe, you were supposed to have turned round and retraced your route which would have brought you back here in the *opposite* direction to the arrow.'

'But, s-sir. I never did get to the end of the universe. I just kept going and going, leaving you further and further behind. Always travelling in the same direction – a straight line. Only, only . . .'

'Only what?'

'Well, I don't know, sir. Suddenly, I saw this crowd ahead of me, and I wondered who they were, and . . . it was *you*! You *weren't* miles and miles behind me as I thought. You were *in front* of me. And . . . and . . . I don't know how you got there – here.' With that, the poor little beetle burst into tears.

'You expect me to believe that drivel?' ranted the professor. 'Confess! As soon as you got out of sight, you altered direction and did a wide loop so you could sneak up behind us.'

'No, no,' whimpered the little fellow. 'I didn't, I really didn't.'

Gedanken was puzzled. To her it sounded as though the driver was being truthful. He was too scared to be otherwise. He *said* he just carried on in the same direction. And sure enough, when he got back, the car *was* lined up with the arrow. But how could he come from the *opposite* direction?

She looked up and scanned the laboratory. A clue somewhere, perhaps? Her eye was drawn to the models on the benches. So many different shapes: a globe, a long horn, a ring-doughnut, a saddle. What could they be for? 'IMAGINARY UNIVERSES LABORATORY'. That's what it had said on the door. A thought occurred to her. 'Surely not. These shapes – could they possibly be some crazed scientist's idea of joke "universes"? I wonder . . .'

Gedanken examined the knobs on the side of the microscope. 'Ah!' she exclaimed as she came across one labelled 'ZOOM'. She grabbed hold of it and peered down the microscope again. She turned the knob – and began to laugh, and laugh. 'Of course. Why didn't I think of it before?'

'And do you know what, Uncle?' she said, on returning to the study. 'You'll never guess. We always thought the rubber sheet was flat – not counting the dimples caused by the pebbles, right? Well, it's not. It's not a flat sheet at all. It's a *globe*! A great big sphere. You can only tell when you zoom out and can take it all in. If you're right close in, like I was to begin with, and like the beetles are all the time, you can't see that it's curved. It looks flat.'

'So you're saying the beetle *did* keep driving in a straight line – a straight line as far as *he* was concerned – in his two dimensions,' said Uncle Albert.

'Yes. But because his path was curved *downwards* – in the third dimension which he couldn't see – he landed back where he started,' added Gedanken triumphantly.

'How interesting,' murmured her uncle. 'How *very* interesting . . . Could just mean . . .'

Gedanken waited expectantly. 'Mean what, Uncle?'

'Could mean the same idea might hold for *our* universe.'

'*Ours*? But how?'

'Well, suppose an astronaut wants to reach the edge of our universe. He goes straight up vertically from the North Pole. He keeps going in a dead straight line. But the next time you see him he appears from *behind* you, and lands vertically on the South Pole.'

'I'd say he cheated. He didn't keep going in a straight line. He nipped round the back of us while he was out of sight.'

'But that's what the professor beetle said.'

'Ah yes, but this is different.'

'Why?'

'Well, the rubber sheet was curved – in the third dimension. In *our* universe, our three-dimensional space hasn't got anoth . . .' Her voiced trailed off.

'Mmmm?' said Uncle Albert, looking at her quizzically. 'Hasn't got another what? We've been through this before, haven't we? I thought we decided there wasn't any need to have a mental picture – a picture of the wonkyness of the three-dimensional space around the Sun, or Earth. Right? So, we don't have to have one of our three-dimensional universe curved back on itself. It's something we can just accept. Yes?'

'You're saying that if someone goes up from the North Pole, and keeps going in a dead straight line – a really truly dead straight line – they will eventually come to the Earth – *ahead* of them? They will land on the South Pole?'

'No, no,' said Uncle Albert hastily, 'I'm not saying that for definite. It's a *possibility*. That's all – just a possibility. It depends.'

'Depends on what?'

'Well, it will depend on how much matter there is in the Universe. Matter curves space, we know that. It curves the space close by. And if you have lots of lumps of matter – lots of galaxies, say – you get lots of local curvatures. They start to overlap with each other and that produces an overall, general curvature.'

'You mean like Mum and Dad in bed?'

Uncle Albert looked uncomfortable. 'What – exactly – do you have in mind?'

'Well Mum's always on at Dad to buy another mattress. Theirs is too soft. They keep landing up in the middle. If there's only one of them, it's all right – there's just one hollow. But with two of them. See what I mean? The *two* hollows next to each other curve the mattress – so they fall in on top of each other.'

Uncle Albert smiled. 'Yes. I suppose that's one way of putting it. And with lots of people in the bed . . . Not that I'm suggesting . . .' he added hastily, looking embarrassed again. 'Well, anyway, I'm sure you get the general drift. The mattress – all curved up at the edges. That's how our space will be. Because of all the matter in it, there will be this general kind of curvature. The question is *how* curved is it? Enough to curve it right back on itself – so an astronaut going in a straight line would land back where he started?'

'Well?' said Gedanken impatiently. '*Is* that the kind of world we live in?'

'We don't know. We just don't know – yet. There are various possibilities, just as there are various possibilities for the two-dimensional world. The rubber sheet could be more or less flat and of a certain definite size – it has a boundary or edge to it. If the beetles crawl in any direction they will get to the edge. Our universe could be the same; it could have an edge to it. If astronauts go off on long journeys, in any direction in three-dimensional space, they'll get to the boundary of our universe. Goodness knows what that would be like. That's why it might be better to think of the Universe as not having a boundary – it goes on for ever. Like a rubber sheet that is infinitely big. Then the astronauts would travel for ever. Or – another possibility – the curvature might be so great as to make the Universe close back on itself. In that case, the Universe wouldn't be infinitely large, but it wouldn't have an edge to it either. That way we don't have to worry about infinity, or what lies beyond the Universe. There is no beyond. That would be *very* satisfactory.'

'How can we find out – which type of universe

ours is?' asked Gedanken.

'We have to count up the matter. The denser the matter, the more curvature and the greater the chance of having a universe that closes back on itself.'

'So why don't we do it? Count it up?' suggested Gedanken eagerly.

'We're trying. We've counted up all the matter we can see, and there's not enough – only about one-tenth what is needed to close the Universe.'

'Oh,' said Gedanken, disappointed. 'So we can't do that funny round trip in a straight line.'

'Hold on. That's the matter we know about – so far. There might be more. Can't tell yet.'

'And what about the expansion of the Universe?' asked Gedanken. 'How does that fit in with this idea of a universe that doubles back on itself?'

'Well, let's see . . .'

'Don't tell me! I've got it! The balloon! The one in the Imaginary Universes Laboratory. I *wondered* what that was for. A balloon being blown up. Right? The beetles' world was round, like a balloon. So all you have to do is imagine it gradually being blown up. It gets bigger, and everything on its surface gets carried away from everything else – just the same as when we thought the sheet was flat.'

Uncle Albert had reached for pen and paper and was busy scribbling. After a while he murmured, '*That's* interesting. The density of matter decides whether the Universe is closed or not. It also decides whether the gravity is strong enough to halt the expansion and bring everything back together again. If there's enough to close it, there's enough to halt the expansion. So that's it, Gedanken. If the space of the Universe closes back on itself, then one day in the future, the expansion of the Universe will stop. After that, everything comes crashing back together.'

'And if there's not enough?' asked Gedanken.

'If there's not enough, it's likely to expand for ever and become infinitely large.'

He looked across at her triumphantly. 'So, that's it. We've wrapped up the Universe. Not bad for a day's work, eh?'

## 5 Bent Light

'You'll never guess what's happened, Uncle,' called out Gedanken over the garden hedge.

Uncle Albert was squatting down by the flower bed doing a spot of weeding. He looked up. 'Well? Go on,' he said impatiently. 'If I'll never guess, there's no point in me trying.'

'I've been on the radio!' she announced.

'The radio?' exclaimed Uncle Albert. He stood up slowly, holding his aching back. 'How did you manage that?'

'Simple really. This morning, Mum had her programme on in the kitchen. She always listens to it – while she's ironing. Real boring it is. I wasn't listening, but I could hear it from the dining room. I was doing my homework – sort of. Anyway, it was that programme where this man comes on half-way through and asks some catch question and if you know the answer you have to phone in quick before the end of the programme. You know the one I mean?'

Uncle Albert shook his head.

'Anyway,' continued Gedanken, coming into the garden to join him, 'the question was quite good.

You had to work out this thing he was thinking of, and he gave two clues. The first was . . . Hold on . . . Yes, that's it: "What ought to be a famous person, but isn't?" And the second was real clever: "What sounds as though it should have a mother and father, but doesn't?"' Gedanken looked at her uncle expectantly. 'Well? Go on. Do you get it?'

Her uncle shrugged his shoulders. 'No idea.'

'But it's easy! A famous person is a star, right? And what *sounds* as though it has a mother and father? It only *sounds* like it.' She waited, but still Uncle Albert looked blank.

'The SUN,' she said. 'Get it? A son has a mother and a father, yes? The Sun, doesn't. S-U-N,' she spelt out, 'sounds like S-O-N, right? And the Sun is a star! *You* told me that. If I hadn't known the Sun was a star, I'd never have got it. Lucky, eh?'

'So, what happened?'

'I told Mum. I told her the answer was the Sun. Wouldn't believe me. But just as I was trying to explain it to her, they repeated the telephone number, so I rang them up. It was a lady at the other end. She told me to hang on a bit, and then I was talking to this David Kendrew bloke – the one on the programme – the one Mum's always on about. And there I was: on the radio! I told him I knew the answer. He asked if Mum had told me it, and I said, "Certainly not. I worked it out for myself." I then told him it was the Sun and I explained all about the Sun being a star and how it was made up of hot gases, and it was in the Galaxy, and our galaxy was only one of lots of galaxies. You know, all that stuff. He said "Very interesting, but we don't have time for all that." And he cut me off! Talk about rude. I told my mum afterwards, I didn't think much of her David Kendrew. But then the lady came back on again – you know, the one who spoke to me first –

and she said "Thank you very much," and she told me they were going to send me a prize of – wait for it – £5. How about that! FIVE QUID for knowing an easy-peasy bit of physics!'

'Well, good for you.' Uncle Albert looked really pleased. 'My famous broadcasting niece.' He knelt down to resume his weeding. 'If you're doing nothing, how about giving me a hand? These weeds are growing like crazy since that rain.'

'Which ones are weeds?' asked Gedanken.

'Not all that sure,' her uncle grinned. 'I work on the principle that if it's growing and looking healthy, pull it out. Bound to be a weed. That's one there . . . so is that . . . and that.'

Gedanken settled down by the side of him and started pulling away.

'Try to get the roots out,' he added. 'Get hold of them low down, close to the ground, before yanking on them. Like this.'

Soon she got the hang of it. Uncle Albert told her that when he did the weeding, he always imagined himself as some great monster uprooting trees and scaring the tiny people hiding under the stones. Somehow, it seemed to Gedanken, her uncle had a way of making everything fun.

After a while, she got to thinking about her recent space trips. 'You know how I went to the Moon the other day. Well, on the way back – before we met up with the Space Shuttle – I dozed off. Dick said I could,' she added hastily. 'There wasn't anything to do at the time. Anyway, when I woke up I was pressed into the back of my seat. I thought, "That's odd. Must have landed already." You see, we were coasting when I went to sleep; I was floating, held by my seat belt. But now it was like being on the launch pad – the craft standing on its end with the nose upwards and me sitting there facing upwards being pulled down into the back of the seat by gravity. So I got up to have a look out of the side window. As I did, I knocked a pencil out of its holder on the control desk. It rolled across the desk to the edge, and then took off behind me for the rear of the craft; it fell to the floor – what we call "the floor" when the craft is on the pad. Didn't think anything to it at the time. But when I got to the window and looked out, there was nothing there! No ground, no nothing. We were still out in empty space miles from anywhere. I thought to myself "What's going on? Where's all this gravity come from?" *Something* must be pulling me down on to the floor. I wouldn't be able to walk across the room otherwise. And the pencil – what made that fall to the floor?'

Uncle Albert looked across at her intently. 'I *think* I know the answer. But go on.'

'Well, it was then I noticed the sound. The rocket motor. Dick had switched the engine on. Correcting our direction home or something. Anyway, he had done it very quietly and gently – not to wake me, I suppose . . .'

'I thought as much,' interrupted Uncle Albert. 'It's this business of acceleration faking gravity again

– what you found out on the Big Dipper. The rocket motor was on and you were speeding up – you were accelerating, and you thought it was gravity because there was no way to tell them apart.' He stopped work, and sat back on the edge of the lawn. 'You know, I reckon we haven't *begun* to think out the consequences of this.'

For a while he just sat there hugging his legs, with his knees tucked up under his chin, lost in thought. 'When you went to sleep, you were coasting along and everything was just floating. What we've been calling "natural" motion. Drifting along in a straight line at a steady speed, or following the natural curves of space if you're close to any heavy objects. But when you woke up, it was no longer natural. Everything was trying to get to the back end of the craft – pencils, you pressed into your seat. Why? What was so special about that end of the craft? Something's going on – something that needs to be *explained*. And we try to explain it by saying the craft is accelerating – it's being pushed on by the rockets placed at that end of the craft. It's accelerating opposite to the direction in which all the loose objects are moving. Or is it?'

'We might be stationary on the launch pad?'

'Right. The launch pad might be in the way, pushing on us from that end to stop us doing the natural thing which is to fall vertically through to the centre of the Earth. Which is the right explanation? We don't know. We know *something* is interfering with the natural motion of the craft, but is this force making us accelerate, or is it stopping us falling under gravity? There's *no way of telling*. No experiment's going to tell acceleration from gravity. They produce the same effects; they're equivalent. In fact,' he said, getting quite excited, 'let's give this idea a name. Let's call it THE EQUIVALENCE PRINCIPLE!'

'Why not THE BIG DIPPER PRINCIPLE?' said Gedanken.

Uncle Albert laughed. 'Call it what you like. I'm a scientist. I have to give it an important-sounding name. Anyway, whatever we call it, I reckon this principle of ours could be useful.'

'How?' asked Gedanken.

'Well, suppose you wanted to find out about very strong gravity – the kind you'd get with a very, very heavy planet or star – but you haven't got such a star handy. You could always fake it – by accelerating hard, in a spacecraft.' He looked at her knowingly. 'See what I mean? What do you reckon? Call it a day out here?'

Gedanken smiled. 'Any special instructions, mission controller?'

'No. Just give it all you've got, and see what happens.'

Back in the spacecraft she found herself weightless, coasting along in empty space. Without losing any time, she leaned forward ready to start up the rocket motors.

But Dick called out. 'Hold on! Before you do that,

notice anything different?'

'Different?' Gedanken replied. She looked about her. 'No. What?'

'There. On the wall next to you. To your left.'

She turned and saw, stuck to the wall of the craft, a card with a series of rings drawn on it. It looked like a target with a bullseye in the middle.

'That? What's it for?' she asked.

'You'll see in a minute. Don't touch. It's lined up with that lamp over there on the other wall,' said Dick.

She looked across and saw a box fixed to the right-hand wall. It had a tube coming out pointing directly at the target.

'That box thing?'

'That's right. It's a ray-gun. Shoots flashes of light. Try it. The switch is in front of you.'

Gedanken scanned the control panel. There was a switch she hadn't noticed before. The label said 'LIGHT GUN'. She reached across and flicked it. Immediately a little beam of light shot out of the barrel of the gun, aimed at the target. It whizzed past Gedanken's face. As it did so, she thought she heard a high-pitched, giggling sort of sound: 'Wheee . . . wheee . . .' Then, as the beam hit the centre of the target, she distinctly heard a triumph-ant little cry: 'Bullseye!' The light beam promptly disappeared. This was followed by a second. Again there was the same kind of voice: 'Wheee . . . wheee . . . Bullseye!' Then another, and another.

Having watched this performance for a while,

Gedanken asked, 'So?'

'Uncle Albert says we're to note what the light beams do, and see if anything changes as we accelerate. So, when you're ready . . .'

Gedanken pressed the big red button in front of her, the rocket engines roared into life, and she felt herself being pushed back into her seat. The craft gathered speed. She kept watch on the light beams. She noticed nothing different: 'Wheee . . . wheee . . . Bullseye!'

Then Gedanken remembered her uncle telling her about really strong gravity; it could be faked by really hard acceleration. So she pressed down on the button more firmly. The noise of the engines grew louder and more urgent. It almost drowned the voices of the pulses – but not quite: 'Wheee . . . wheee . . . oops!' 'Wheee . . . wheee . . . oops!'

To Gedanken's surprise, she noticed that the beams were now missing the bullseye. Not by much, but they were definitely arriving off-centre. They were hitting a point slightly shifted towards the back end of the craft. There were also more voices. As well as the despairing cries of 'oops!' from the light beams, she could now hear a muffled, mocking chant coming from the ray-gun box: 'Yah, yer missed! What a load of rubbish! Yah, yer missed! What a load of rubbish!'

'Must be the other light beams waiting their turn,' she thought. 'How unkind.'

She decided she would teach them a lesson. She pressed the button with all her strength. The engine noise became deafening. But not so deafening that she couldn't make out the anguished cries of: 'Wheee . . . Oh no . . . Ouch!' 'Wheee . . . Hey, not fair . . . Ouch!' 'Wheee . . . Oi, keep still . . . Ouch!'

The little light beams curved through the air, just missing Gedanken's nose, and hit the outermost ring of the target! As with the first beams, they were landing on the side of the bullseye closest to the rear of the craft. It was as though something was pulling them towards that end of the cabin. The greater the acceleration, the bigger the effect.

She took her finger off the button. The engines stopped. Again the craft coasted along and she became weightless once more.

'Wheee . . . that's better . . . Bullseye!' The beams were again hitting the centre of the target.

Gedanken sat there thinking. What on Earth was going on? Running through her mind were the earlier protests from the light beams: 'Not fair'; 'Keep still'. What could they have meant? Now that she was coasting again, everything had gone back to normal – what Uncle Albert called the 'natural' state to be in. Good sensible behaviour. Everything staying where it is, and light rays moving in straight lines. The ray-gun points to the bullseye, so the light beams hit the bullseye. But then with the engines on – with the craft accelerating – it all goes crazy. Light beams go in a curved path. 'But hold on,' she thought. 'It looked curved to *me*. But how did it look to the light beams? They weren't accelerating like me. They couldn't have been. They weren't fixed to the cabin – not while they were going across from one side to the other. So they must have thought they were still going in a straight line heading for the bullseye. But then . . . Why, of course . . . That's it! I've got it! They were heading for the bullseye to begin with, but then the target started to accelerate – it speeded up. While the beam was going from right to left, the target *moved forward*. The beam carried on in a straight line, and hit the point where the bullseye *ought* to have been. But the bullseye wasn't there any more because it had moved. "Not fair",

"Keep still". Yes, of course, that's it.'

Excitedly, she explained all this to Dick, but he didn't seem terribly interested. 'Well, I bet Uncle Albert will be impressed,' she said. 'Anyway, Dick, do a sum for me. Work out how far the cabin and the target and everything moved forward while the beam crossed from the gun to the target. I mean how far extra it moved because it was accelerating.'

Dick came up with the answer: '25 centimetres.'

'And how big is this target?' she asked.

'How big?'

'The outer ring – where the beams were landing just now? How far is it from the bullseye?'

'Er, 25 centimetres,' said Dick.

'There you are! What did I say? They're the same. The light beams say the target moved forward 25 centimetres; I say they curved through the air by 25 centimetres. Any way you look at it, the beams miss the bullseye and hit the outer ring. That solves it! Mission completed. Beam me down, please.'

She was right. Uncle Albert was *very* impressed. 'Of course, you know what this means,' he said. 'This holds for gravity as well as acceleration. The Equivalence Principle, and all that.'

'Go on,' she said.

'Well. You were accelerating and the light beams got curved, right? You were sitting in your seat, pressed back by the acceleration, and you saw the light beams curve. Right, well, the Principle says that if you were sitting in your seat pressed back by *gravity* – because you were on the launch pad with the nose cone pointing upwards – the same thing would happen. You would see the light beams curve in exactly the same way. Not only are you pulled downwards into the back of your seat, *the light beams will be pulled downwards too.'*

Gedanken was not convinced. 'But that's not what light does. The light from over there,' she said, nodding in the direction of the window, 'that's in gravity, but it's not being pulled down or anything.'

'Ah, but that's just the Earth's gravity. It's not very strong. It would have to be *much* stronger than that to see light curve. Like when you first started accelerating: the beams still hit the bullseye – more or less. You couldn't see that really they were arriving ever so slightly off-centre. Same with gravity. Light *always* tends to curve downwards, but usually we don't see it.'

'But we know it's there because of the Principle?'

Uncle Albert nodded.

'Hmmm,' she added thoughtfully, 'Has this got anything to do with wonky space? Gravity bends space, right? Jellies and all that. And Space Shuttles go in curves because space is curved. Is that why light goes in curves?'

Uncle Albert smiled broadly, 'Spot on.'

'Are there any places in the Universe where gravity *is* strong? I mean *really* strong. Things would look funny, wouldn't they? I mean, the light coming from them would be bent – as if it had gone through crinkly glass – like you get in bathroom windows. And . . . Hey . . . I've just thought. If we lived on a very, very heavy planet . . .' She burst out laughing.

'Yes? Go on,' encouraged Uncle Albert.

'Well, all the light would end up on the floor! Wouldn't it? The light from that window wouldn't be able to get across the room. It would start out trying to reach us, but then get pulled on to the floor.'

Uncle Albert frowned. 'Yes,' he murmured after a

while. 'I guess that must be right. In *very* strong gravity . . . light . . . in fact, *everything* . . . absolutely everything . . . What a thought. The floor – the planet – would be like a hole in space – a hole that sucked in anything and everything that came within range.'

'Like a vacuum cleaner?' suggested Gedanken.

'You could call it that. A vacuum cleaner in space. Nothing would ever be able to get out of it. Not even light that tried to move directly outwards. And that would mean . . . if no light came from it, it would look – black.'

'Wow! That's great,' exclaimed Gedanken. 'Let's call it . . . Yes, why don't we call it a BLACK HOLE. A black hole in space. Brilliant, eh?' Then she added, 'Do they exist? Black holes – is there such a thing, Uncle?'

Uncle Albert shrugged. 'Don't know. Could be, I suppose.'

'I'll go and look for one,' she said eagerly. 'Beam me up and I'll take a look round the Universe for you.'

'You'll do nothing of the sort,' said her uncle firmly.

'Why not? Don't you want to find out. *I* do!' she declared.

'It's not that easy. In the first place, how do you expect to see one? It swallows up light; it doesn't reflect it, or give out any of its own. So there's nothing to see. And secondly . . .' He got up out of his chair and beckoned to Gedanken. She rose and came over to him.

'And secondly,' he continued, 'it's dangerous. It swallows up everything within range and never lets go of them!' With this, he suddenly threw his arms round her and hugged her so tight she could hardly breathe.

'Lemme go!' she squealed. 'LET GO – OR I'LL TICKLE!'

# 6 Children Older than Parents

'Hi,' greeted Uncle Albert.

Gedanken swept in without a word. He closed the front door behind her. 'Don't I get a kiss today?'

She went back and gave him a light peck on the cheek.

'Anything the matter?' he asked.

She shrugged.

'Coffee? I'm just making some,' he suggested.

'Don't mind,' she replied glumly.

As he led the way to the kitchen and put the kettle on, he muttered, 'Sounds as though someone got out of bed the wrong . . .'

'If you must know, I had a rotten time last night,' she said sulkily. 'There's been a terrible row.'

'Oh? Who between?'

'Between everybody and Jeremy.'

'Huh. Not surprised. What's he been up to now?'

'It was the gig last night, right? At the youth club. Remember? I told you. It was all going fine, when Jeremy started his dirty tricks.'

'Dirty tricks?'

'Tracy told me about it. Tracy on drums, you know? She said Jeremy turns his amp up – so his

94

guitar sounds louder than the rest of them. Does it when he thinks no one's looking. You sort out the settings at the rehearsals. But then he goes and turns his up during the gig! Big show-off! "It's *my* band, *my* band." Well, it's *not* his band. Not really. It's *ours*, isn't it?'

Uncle Albert looked as if he didn't want to get involved.

'Well, it *is*,' said Gedanken firmly. 'Anyway, I don't want to talk about it.'

'Good. Just remember, any time you need a lead violin . . .'

'You must be joking!' she exploded – but she couldn't help smiling to herself.

Uncle Albert made the drinks and got out the biscuit tin. 'You could help with the jigsaw next door, if you like. Might take your mind off things.'

She wandered through to the study and whiled away ten minutes putting in the few remaining border pieces. But when that was complete, it got more difficult and she lost interest. Too much sky anyway.

'Tell you what, Uncle. There *is* something I fancy doing,' she called out.

'Oh? What's that?' asked Uncle Albert, coming in to join her.

'I could go hunting for a black hole,' she said, looking at him expectantly. 'That might cheer me up.'

'You know what I think about that. We still don't know enough about them. Until we do, it's much too risky to send you near one. Much safer to stick to what we're doing.'

'Meaning?'

'Meaning we carry on faking strong gravity by hard acceleration. We can control how hard we accelerate; we can't control black holes.'

'But *sometime* I'm going to be able to look for one, aren't I? When we've learned everything.'

'We'll see. Not promising anything.'

'Anyway, what more is there to learn?' asked Gedanken. 'We already know what it's like to accelerate hard.'

'Not sure. But there might be something,' Uncle Albert said, settling into his favourite chair. He began thoughtfully stroking his chin. The bubble took shape above his head . . .

'Hey, Dick. Where's the ray-gun gone?' she asked, looking to where it used to be on the side wall.

'It's been moved. Front of the cabin – straight ahead of you, on the floor,' answered Dick.

'Oh, yes. What's it sitting on – that box thing with the zero numbers on?' she asked.

'That? It's a clock. A digital clock,' explained Dick. 'Starts at zero and counts the seconds. It controls the ray-gun so as to give out a flash every second.'

'What for?'

'Don't ask me. How should I know? There's another behind you.'

Gedanken swivelled round in her seat. Sure enough, a second ray-gun and clock, identical to the first, were set up against the back wall.

'Uncle Albert says you're to keep an eye on them,' continued Dick. 'The light switch on the control panel operates both now. That way they start together. You're to go ahead whenever you like.'

Gedanken flicked the switch and both ray-guns immediately gave out a flash of light. This was repeated each second. At the same time the digital read-outs displayed the number of pulses given out: 1, 2, 3, . . . Gedanken noted that they kept pace with each other, both showing the same number.

'Right, Dick,' she said. 'We have to start accelerating now, do we?'

'That's right, Captain.'

She pushed the red button. The rocket engines roared. She was pressed back into her seat as the craft began to speed up. She looked around her. Nothing unusual – clocks behaving as before, keeping good time and continuing to emit their light beams. She pushed harder on the button; the engines responded. She was now being uncomfortably pushed into her seat. Still nothing unusual . . . except . . . hold on. The light coming from the clock in front of her. It had a blue tinge to it. Gedanken was puzzled. She could have sworn the light had been yellow – pure yellow. Not only that, but the beams appeared to be coming at a faster rate now – more than once a second. She couldn't be sure; it was hard to judge. But it certainly seemed that way.

She turned to look at the rear clock. It wasn't easy.

The high rate of acceleration strained her neck muscles. She managed it though – and got another surprise. The light from this clock had turned red! Yes, it was definitely red. And, unlike the first clock, this one appeared to have slowed down!

She quickly looked from one clock to the other. There was no doubt about it. The one at the front was sending out beams at a faster rate than the one at the rear. The blue beams from the front, as they passed her, called out excitedly 'Wheee . . . here already!' 'Wheee . . . I'm turbo-charged!' Not so the red ones from the back. They grumbled 'Phew . . . about time too . . . where do you think you were going?' 'Phew . . . not fair . . . thought I'd never make it.'

Gedanken let go the button. She sat there pondering this latest mystery. Everything was back to normal again now. Both beams were yellow, and they were arriving at the same rate. Except that not quite *everything* was back to normal. The clocks were now out of step! Whereas earlier they had agreed with each other, now they didn't. The front one read 358, the rear 336. A little later: 375 and 353. Then: 392 and 370. Always the rear one lagged behind the front one by 22 seconds.

'I thought so,' said Gedanken. 'The front one *was* going faster than the back one. Did you notice, Dick? The acceleration knackered the clocks.'

'Um,' murmured Dick. 'Not so sure of that. They were certainly going at different rates. I noticed that. That's why I did a check on them. But they seemed to be working normally – quite normally. No faults, no nothing. Except that one was like a film speeded up; the other was slowed down.'

Gedanken found this all very puzzling. But then she remembered the light beams and what they had said as they had passed her: 'Not fair.' 'Where do you think you were going?' Going? Who were they talking about? Herself? *She* hadn't been going any-where. She had been sitting still in her seat. But wait a minute. She had been accelerating. The craft and everything in it had accelerated. At least, everything fixed to the craft. The beams hadn't accelerated – not while they were on their journey from the lamp to herself. But she had accelerated – away from the beams coming from the back. So what would that mean?

She thought hard. It was all very difficult. But she didn't want Uncle Albert explaining it to her when she got back if she could work it out for herself.

'When I'm coasting like this – in the natural state,' she argued, 'the beams go a certain distance to reach me. So they ought to arrive after a certain time. But if as soon as the beam starts its journey I accelerate, then . . . by the time the beam arrives at the point where it expected to meet up with me . . . why, of course! I won't be there any more! I'd be further away – because of the acceleration. It's the business of the target all over again. The target moved from where the beams thought it was going to be. Now it's me that's the target. Great! So, how does that work out? I moved *away* from the beam, right? So, I had further to go. That means it took longer to get to me. Same with the second beam pulse – the one behind the first. That had even further to go. And that means the beams arrive spread out. Yes, that's it. They arrive spread out. And that means they arrive at a slower rate!'

Gedanken was thrilled. And of course, it took her no time to work out that precisely the opposite would apply to the beams coming at her from the front of the craft. Her acceleration took her *towards* these beams, so they would have *less* distance to travel than normal. They would therefore be bunched up and arrive at a *faster* rate.

'Oh boy! Is Uncle Albert going to *love* this!'

She was right. Uncle Albert was thrilled. 'Marvellous! An excellent piece of scientific observation. And as for your explanation – couldn't have done better myself,' he said.

'OK, OK, Uncle, that explains the different rates,' said Gedanken. 'But what about the colours? What I don't understand is why the front beams went blue, and the others red?'

'Same reason as before,' he said.

'How?'

'Well, light is made up of waves. You know that, don't you?'

Gedanken nodded, though she wasn't really sure.

'So,' he continued, 'each pulse of light is made up of a short series of humps and dips – a bit like the water ripples you get when you drop the soap into the bath. When you accelerated towards the light coming from the front, you met up with the humps and dips faster – they appeared to be squashed up together. Not only did the one-second pulses appear to be closer to each other, but the humps and dips of each of those pulses – they too were closer to each other. And as for the light coming from the rear, the same sort of thing happened – only the other way round: for them the humps and dips were spread out.'

'But what's all this humping and dipping got to do with the colour of the light?' Gedanken insisted.

'I'm trying to explain! The difference between the colours is all to do with the distances between the humps and dips. For blue light they're close together, for red they're wider apart. Yellow is in between. So, if you start with yellow light and accelerate towards it, you turn it blue; accelerate away, and it goes red.'

'But I still don't see what the distance between humps and dips has got to do with colour? What's *blue* about squashed-up humps and dips, and *red* about spread-out ones? I don't get it.'

Uncle Albert smiled, 'Well, frankly, I don't either. No one does. It's just the way it is. It's the same with sound. Yes, take sound. That's also made up of waves. But there, the distance between the humps and dips is all to do with the pitch of the note – the note that we hear. Again we don't know why – why the distance between the humps should govern the note. It just does. The further apart the humps, the lower the note. And just as with light you can change one colour into another by your motion, so you can change one note into another. Take the siren on a police car. It comes towards you, the humps get squashed together, and the note sounds higher. The car goes past, the siren goes away from you, the humps are now stretched out, and the note sounds lower. You *must* have heard that. "Pitch-bending", I believe you keyboard players call it,' he added with a twinkle in his eye.

She smiled. 'Oh. So, you're saying that when I saw the colours change, that was like what happens to the police siren.'

'Yes, that's right. Changing the colour of light, changing the pitch of a sound – it's the same thing. It's all to do with squashing up waves and spreading them out.'

'Yes, but that means – if that desk light was on – and I got up and started to accelerate towards it, the light goes blue. But it doesn't.'

'Hold on,' said her uncle. 'I didn't quite say that. Strictly speaking, yes, it would tend to go blue – ever so slightly. But you'd never notice it – not with the kind of acceleration you could manage. In practice, to turn yellow into blue, you'd have to accelerate ... oooh ... I'd say something like a hundred million million times harder than anything you're likely to do in normal everyday life. The effect is always there, but you'd never detect it. That's why you didn't notice anything in the spacecraft until you accelerated really hard ...' He stopped.

Gedanken waited for him to carry on. But he didn't.

'What is it, Uncle?' she asked.

'Hmmm,' replied Uncle Albert slowly. 'Of course. We've been overlooking ...'

'What?' she interrupted impatiently. 'What have we been overlooking?'

'The purpose of your mission. You went up there not to investigate what happens when you accelerate. But to find out what happens in strong gravity. Everything you've found out for acceleration applies to gravity as well.'

'The Big Dipper, and all that,' said Gedanken.

Uncle Albert nodded. 'If the craft was sitting on a launch pad – nose cone upwards – and if it was on a planet where the gravity was really powerful, so you were pulled back into your seat exactly the way you were when you were accelerating hard ...'

'The light from the nose cone would turn blue,' exclaimed Gedanken. 'And the other would go red – the light from behind me – er, or is it below me?'

'That's right. In gravity, you would get blue light from above you and red light from below.'

'And the stronger the gravity, the bluer and redder they would be?' asked Gedanken. Uncle Albert nodded.

'But,' she continued, 'the clocks – would they go wrong in gravity? They got out of step when I accelerated hard, remember? So would that happen in gravity too?'

Uncle Albert just looked at her, as if waiting for her to go on.

'They would, wouldn't they?' she said. 'They must do. The Principle says so . . . so it would . . . right?'

'That's my girl! You're catching on.'

'So, that's it: gravity knackers clocks.'

'Hey, hey. Not so fast. I didn't say *that*,' Uncle Albert said hurriedly. 'Dick was right. The clocks work normally – perfectly normally, whether they're accelerating or in strong gravity. It's *time itself* that is affected. That's the important thing. *Time itself* is affected by gravity. It runs slower low down compared to what it does higher up. That's what you've just discovered.'

'But that's crazy,' said Gedanken. 'You're saying that in a building – a skyscraper, say – on the top floor, the clocks go faster than those on the ground floor!'

'Yes. That's what I'm saying. Mind you, if you were on the top floor, you wouldn't think your clocks up there were going fast. It is time that has speeded up, so *everything* gets speeded up – not just the clocks – but your heart-beat, your breathing, the rate at which your brain ticks over, and so the rate at which you think. A clock that's going fast, looked at by someone whose mind is churning over faster by the same amount, seems to be going at the normal rate!'

Gedanken thought about this for a while. Uncle Albert watched her with amusement. For a moment she wished she were on the top floor of a very, very high skyscraper. That way she could speed up her thinking. She'd put her uncle in the basement so that *his* brain would go slow, for a change. It would then be *her* turn to be the genius! She rather liked that.

'Tell me,' she said, 'if I'm on the top floor, I think my clock is OK, right? But suppose I look at a clock on the ground floor – through binoculars, say. With my fast brain, will I see the one down there going slow?'

'Yes. You'll see everything happening slowly down there. It's all very sluggish.'

'And someone down there . . .?'

'He'll think everything on the ground floor is normal. Slow clocks look OK to slow brains. But when he looks up at what's happening on the top floor, he sees everything speeded up. Life is frantic up there.'

'So,' said Gedanken, 'everyone thinks their own

life is normal, and it's the other's that's gone wrong – going too fast or too slow. But who's right? Who is *really* normal? They can't both be.'

'But they can. There's no way to choose between them. One is fast *relative* to the other, or slow *relative* to the other – and that's all that can be said.'

'It all sounds very muddly,' said Gedanken. 'Does this mean when I go upstairs to bed, I ought to reset my watch when I come down in the morning – because it's got out of step with the clocks down-stairs?'

Uncle Albert chuckled. 'Strictly speaking, yes. But I shouldn't bother if I were you. In the Earth's gra-vity you'd only have to alter it by . . .' He paused to do some more mental arithmetic. '. . . yes, by about one second in every 100 million years you spent up there.'

'That's all!' exclaimed Gedanken. 'Huh. Not worth finding out, was it?'

'I wouldn't say that,' replied Uncle Albert firmly. 'It's important to know that this is going on under our noses. The effects may be small here, but per-haps not everywhere. There might be places in the Universe where you could play some very interest-ing games.'

'What do you mean?'

'Well, suppose you were on a planet with very, very strong gravity. Suppose you lived at the top of the building, and your parents stayed on the ground floor. Time for you goes faster than theirs, right? Your birthdays come round faster than theirs. So . . .'

He broke off and looked at her encouragingly.

She thought for a moment, and then began to laugh. 'No, you're kidding!' she exclaimed in wide-eyed astonishment. 'I'd get older than them! Hey. That would be great. I could then do whatever I wanted to. It would be *my* turn to get the good stuff. I'd get a brand new keyboard and Dad would have to make do with an old car – one that was always going wrong and making him embarrassed in front of his friends. How about that!'

# 7 The Black Hole

'Uncle!' Gedanken called out. 'Wait for me.'

Uncle Albert was struggling down the garden path carrying a heavy shopping bag.

'You timed that well,' he grunted. 'Could have done with your help sooner. Here, take this,' he said, handing her the bag. He flexed his fingers to get the feeling back, and fumbled in his pocket for his keys. 'That supermarket! Always end up buying too much.'

As soon as they were inside, Gedanken made her announcement. 'Uncle, you'll never guess what's happened.'

'You've been on the radio again.'

'How did you know?' she demanded crossly, dumping the bag down.

'Didn't. It just seems to be a conversation we've had before. Why? *Have* you been on again?'

'Not exactly. But I am going to be. Properly this time. In the studio and all that.'

'You're kidding.'

'No. It's true. And do you know what? This time I'll be on the CHRIS PARKER show!'

Uncle Albert looked blank.

She stared at him in disbelief. 'You've never heard of him, have you,' she said. Uncle Albert shook his head.

'Really, Uncle,' she said in disgust. '*Everyone* listens to the Chris Parker show. You ask at school.' Then she added patiently, 'He's a DJ. You've heard of DJs, right? Well he is THE DJ of Radio Beacon. Radio Beacon – the local station – OK? Well, I'm being interviewed . . .'

'*Interviewed*!' he declared in astonishment. 'What does he want to interview *you* for?!'

'Well, why shouldn't he?' she said defiantly. 'He interviews all the others.'

'What others?'

'Teenagers. On Tuesday nights at seven. Local teenagers – in between the music. You get to say "Hi!" to your friends.'

'Is that all? Hi!'

'Of course not. You only get on if you've got something specially interesting to say – about the news or what you've been doing.'

'And what will *you* be saying?' he asked.

'Well . . .' she said uncertainly, 'they want me to talk about our research – into space and time and all that.'

'Really?' said Uncle Albert, beginning to take an interest. 'That's great. But . . .' He looked puzzled. 'How did they get to hear about that?'

'I told Susan,' she replied.

'Susan?'

'The lady I spoke to that first time I rang up. The

one who told me about the five quid. Well, we got talking, you see. She said she had always been interested in science, but had been put off because everyone told her it wasn't for girls, only boys. And she hoped I wouldn't be put off like she was. I said I wasn't going to be, and I was already doing scientific research with you. So, that was that, I thought. But then, this morning she rings back to say I'm on the Chris Parker show.'

'But I thought she was with the other programme.'

'Yes, she is. But she also helps out with the Chris Parker show. And she had talked to him about me.'

'Well,' said Uncle Albert. 'That's terrific. The Chris Parker show, eh. Must be sure to listen – I'll tell my friends. *Next* Tuesday, is it?'

Gedanken nodded. It was then he noticed that she looked a little worried, as well as excited. He asked if anything was the matter.

She shrugged. 'People don't normally talk about science on that show. They might think I'm boring – or showing off, or something. The boys'll think I'm just a swot. A real wimp.'

'*The* Number One DJ wants you on his show.'

'But *does* he?' she asked. 'I forget what this Susan woman said exactly, but it sounded to me as though Chris Parker didn't like the idea at first. Besides. Suppose he asks me questions I can't answer?'

'We'll just have to make sure you *do* know the answers.'

On reaching the study, Uncle Albert settled into

his chair, removed his shoes, and wiggled his toes. 'Ah, that's better,' he said.

Gedanken stared at his bare feet. 'Uncle, why is it you never wear socks?'

'Socks? Why should I? They'd only get holes in them. Besides, they'd get dirty and smelly and need washing. This way, I only have to wash my feet.'

Gedanken smiled. She couldn't wait to become famous so she too could do sensible things like that without getting picked on.

Just then a mischievous look came into her eye. 'Uncle,' she said slowly, 'there was something I meant to ask you. These black holes. Chris Parker's bound to ask lots of questions about them – because they're really interesting. You know ... Do they exist? ... What's it like to go inside one? ... That sort of thing. And I don't know what to say. Do you?'

Uncle Albert shifted uncomfortably in his seat. He shook his head.

'I thought not,' she said. 'So. How about it?'

'How about what?'

'You *know* what. I've got to go and find a black hole, haven't I?'

Uncle Albert stroked his chin. For a long time he said nothing. He just stared at his outstretched feet. Gedanken waited and waited.

Eventually he broke the silence. 'I don't know, Gedanken. I'm not at all happy about it. It's *so* risky. If something went wrong and you landed up *inside* a black hole, I'd never be able to get you out. At least I don't think I could. Physically – out there in the *real* world – it would be quite impossible. Whether it could be done with the thought-bubble ... I've never used it before to think of impossible things – not things that are *absolutely* impossible . . .'

'I'd be ever so careful,' Gedanken said. 'I promise to do whatever you say.'

'Well,' said Uncle Albert hesitantly, 'it would certainly cap everything we've been doing if you did find a black hole. In fact, I've been thinking. You know how I said you could never see one – because it doesn't give out any light? Well, it might not be so difficult after all. You'd still be able to see things approaching it – clouds of dust, that sort of thing. You'd see them being sucked into some kind of centre and disappearing . . .'

'The vacuum cleaner idea,' said Gedanken eagerly.

'That's right. I also reckon I know where to look for one.'

Rather against his will, the thought-bubble had begun to appear.

'Go on,' said Gedanken encouragingly.

'Well,' said Uncle Albert, 'I was thinking about very old stars – burnt-out ones. They don't have the energy to hold themselves up any longer – against their own gravitational forces. So all the stuff of the star collapses into the middle. And with all that stuff packed into a tiny space, gravity would become very, very strong . . .'

'Strong enough to make a black hole?' asked Gedanken.

'Possibly. If the star was heavy enough. If it weren't, the star would collapse down to a certain size and then stay like that. But with a very, very heavy star – several times heavier than the Sun – the gravity would be so strong, nothing would be able to resist it. It would swallow up the whole star.'

He rose from his seat and began pacing up and down. 'Then there's another possibility,' he continued, gradually getting more and more worked up. 'There could be a black hole at the centre of a galaxy. Remember how the stars go round and round the centre of their galaxy? It's their motion that keeps them apart? Well, perhaps some don't go fast enough – they fall to the centre. Just think: Stars piling in on top of each other. There could be millions of them – hundreds of millions – *thousands* of millions of stars all swallowed up in the one hole.'

Gedanken's eyes shone with excitement. 'That's the one for me!' she said.

Eagerly she watched him go back and forth, back and forth, the thought-bubble getting brighter and clearer all the time.

After what seemed an age, he suddenly declared, 'Right. I've decided. You can go.'

'UNCLE!' she squealed, and rushed over to give him a big hug. 'Wonderful!' she cried.

'All right, all right. Stop that. Can't have you too excited. This is no ordinary trip. You've *got* to obey instructions – to the letter. Is that understood?'

'Yes, Uncle,' she promised. 'I'll be good – ever so good.'

'OK,' he said, returning to his chair and signalling to her to sit opposite. 'I'll beam you up to a point in space close to the centre of a galaxy. I want you to look for anything unusual – anything that could be due to a black hole. But if you find it, under NO circumstances get too close to it. Anything that crosses the boundary of a black hole cannot get back. Things can go in, but nothing can get out. Is that clear!'

'Yes, Uncle,' she said. 'I shall remember.'

Arriving in the spacecraft she was greeted by Dick. 'Good afternoon, Captain.' He sounded serious.

'Hi, Dick,' she replied cheerily. 'How about it then? Got him to agree to it at last. Great, eh?'

'If you say so.'

'What's the matter? You don't sound very excited.'

'Should I be?'

'Well, why not? We're going to visit a black hole.'

'Huh!'

Gedanken decided to ignore his grumpiness. He was obviously in a mood.

'Where are we? Can you see anything?' she asked.

'Take a look for yourself. Out of the side window, to the left. I don't like it. Not one little bit,' Dick said.

What a sight! She could hardly believe it. There

outside was what seemed to be a gigantic whirlpool. Clouds of dust swirling around and slowly being sucked into the middle – like bath water going down a plug-hole.

'Wow!' she cried. 'Do you think that's *it*? In the middle there. Do you think that's a black hole, Dick?'

'Don't know,' he said. 'But I don't like it.'

As she watched, more and more clouds and pebbles and rocks were being pulled into the middle. As they got closer to the centre they appeared to change colour. They went red.

'Gravity,' she exclaimed. 'I bet that's it. I bet anything you like gravity is really strong in there.'

As fast as the stuff disappeared into the centre so, on the far outside of the whirlpool, more and more of the dust clouds of outer space were captured and began their journey inwards – slowly at first, but always getting faster and faster.

'Captain,' interrupted Dick. 'Sorry, but we really must do something. We're falling towards that thing.'

'Hey, you're right,' agreed Gedanken. 'We *are* closer, aren't we. Hadn't noticed that. What do we do?'

'I'll turn the craft so the rockets are pointing towards the hole.'

There was a soft purring sound as the small directional side-rockets rotated the craft.

'Right,' said Dick. 'That's fine. Now start up the

main motors and our rocket thrust will counteract gravity.'

Gedanken pressed the red button, and the rockets started up.

'How's that?' she asked.

'One moment,' said Dick. 'No. Give it a bit more.'

She pressed harder. 'Like this?'

A pause, then Dick said 'Yes. That's OK. We're more or less stationary now.' He sounded relieved.

'Good,' said Gedanken. 'Can I let go now?'

'NO! NO!' Dick cried. 'Of course not. You have to keep the engines going. Switch off and we shall start falling again. As long as we stay this close to the hole we have to keep the rocket thrust going.'

Having to hold the button down all the time made it a bit awkward for looking out of the side window, but by craning her neck she could just manage to see the hole to the rear of the craft.

Suddenly, she was blinded! A dazzling fiery ball as bright as the Sun came into view. It was a star. She had to turn away. By the time she dared take another look – this time squinting through almost closed eyes – the star's appearance had completely changed. It was now red and had become quite dull. It was plunging in the direction of the hole. As she watched, it rapidly grew fainter and fainter. That was strange enough. But then she noticed something *very* peculiar. As the star got closer to the hole, it slowed down. Yes. There was no doubt about it. As it approached the boundary of the hole, it slowed down, until it eventually came to a halt! A complete standstill. It just stayed where it was. Mind you, Gedanken couldn't see it for long. The light went a very deep, faint red, and then quickly disappeared altogether. It was as though the light of the star had been switched off. But although she could no longer see anything, she could swear that the star stopped on the edge of the hole and did not go in!

'Did you see that, Dick?' she asked.

'Yes,' he replied.

'I reckon Uncle's got it wrong. That star stopped. Quite definitely stopped. It did not go in.'

'He's not often wrong,' Dick pointed out.

'We all make mistakes,' said Gedanken. 'That's what Uncle says. I reckon we ought to go and investigate.'

'Your promise, Gedanken. You promised Uncle Albert not to get too close,' Dick reminded her.

'I know that, Dick. But we're scientists. It's our job to find things out.'

'Well, I don't know,' said Dick, obviously very worried. 'We have our orders.'

'Yes, but when he gave those orders, he didn't know what *we* know – about something stopping you from going in. It's like that wire-mesh barrier thing – the one he told me about – the one that stops boats at the last moment from going over the weir. If something stopped the star going in, it'll stop us. Won't it?'

Dick didn't reply. It was then she remembered how he had once called her 'chicken' – the time he wanted to go somewhere else when she was under orders to go to the Moon. He didn't mind then about disobeying orders. That decided her. She'd show him who was really chicken. Screwing up her courage, she deliberately took her finger off the button. The sound of the rocket motors died away. Immediately they resumed their fall towards the hole.

'Oh, no,' moaned Dick. 'What *are* you doing? For goodness sake . . .'

'Stop fussing. We'll just go to where the star stopped. As soon as we get there, I'll start up the motors again.'

Gedanken continued to look intently out of the window in the direction of the black hole. Still she could see no star. 'That's funny,' she thought after a while. 'Could swear we ought to have caught up with it by now. It wasn't all that far below us when it stopped.'

'See anything, Dick?' she said.

'Yes. A heap of trouble.'

'I mean the star.'

'No, I can't. As far as I can make out, we've already passed where it's *supposed* to have stopped. I reckon we've crossed the boundary and are now *inside* the hole.'

At these words, Gedanken felt a chill run down her spine. 'Stop it!' she demanded. 'You're just trying to frighten me. There's no hole out there. Everything's quite normal. We haven't crossed any boundary or anything. There wasn't any bump.'

'There's no bump when you go over the equator. What's that supposed to prove?' said Dick.

'Well, we'll soon see who's right,' said Gedanken. She pressed the red button – all the way. She was slammed into the back of her seat. The noise of the rockets was deafening. Outside everything flashed past the window – dust, pebbles, light beams – all on their way to the centre of the black hole.

'How's that?' called out Gedanken. 'We're on our way out – aren't we?'

Dick said something, but she couldn't catch it over the din from the engines.

'What was that?' she cried.

'I said,' shouted Dick, 'We're *not* on our way out. We're still being pulled towards the centre of the hole.'

'Can't be,' protested Gedanken. Her hair tingled. 'Give me more power.'

'We're already on top overdrive. There's nothing more to give you.'

Top overdrive! That's almost infinite thrust! The maximum power of the most powerful rocket imaginable – and still not enough. Gedanken's tummy turned over as the awful truth dawned on her. She had gone too far. She had never been so scared in all her life.

'Dick, Dick,' she called out. 'What shall we do?'

'What was that?'

'I said . . .'

'No good. Can't hear. The noise. You'll have to switch off the engines.'

She hesitated – but then realized the rocket was useless anyway. She let go the button. All became quiet again.

'That's better,' said the computer. 'So. I hope you're satisfied. You can't say I didn't warn you.'

'Huh, clever dick,' Gedanken snorted.

'Hardly the time for compliments, but thanks all the same.'

'Oh stop it, Dick. I'm frightened. What's going to happen now?'

'Don't know. But with everything heading for the centre of the hole, I imagine there's going to be an almighty crash when we get there. You'd better try and get ready for it. Lie out straight with your feet pointing towards the centre of the hole – that's towards the rear of the craft. Brace yourself for the impact. It might help. But then again, probably not.'

She did as she was told. It was then she became aware of something very strange. As she lay there floating in space, she felt herself being stretched. It was as though something had got hold of her feet and was trying to pull them. At the same time she could feel her neck muscles being strained. Her head was being pulled in the opposite direction. There was no doubt about it. She was being stretched! Not only that, but she noticed her arms being drawn into her sides. Her body felt as if it were being wrapped in very, very tight bandages. She told Dick.

'Same must be happening to me,' he said. At least, she assumed it was Dick who spoke. It cer-

tainly didn't sound like him. The voice was low –
more like a growl.

'Why are you talking funny?' she asked.

'Can't help it. Some power units out of action . . .
connections . . . pulled out.'

Gedanken felt the tears beginning to come. 'Call
for help, Dick,' she choked. 'Send a radio message.'

'Can't,' replied the computer. 'Impossible . . .
Black hole . . . nothing gets out.'

'Then send some other kind of message.'

'Impossible . . . *nothing* gets out . . . We're cut
off . . .'

The stretching became unbearable. 'Dick, I'm
frightened.'

' . . . Gedanken . . .'

'Yes?'

' . . . Gedanken . . . good . . . bye . . .'

'Dick! DICK! Don't go! Are you there?'

Silence. The lights on the control panel went out.
The TV monitors went dead. She was alone. A wave
of panic seized her. She began to sob and moan. She
was now in such pain, and moment by moment it
got worse. From all around her came creaking and
groaning noises. The walls of the craft began to
buckle under the same kind of sideways force that
was pressing in on her body. There were metallic
twanging sounds.

All sorts of thoughts began to race through her
mind. The rowing boat near the weir – only this time
they had gone too far and Uncle Albert was not
strong enough to row them back to safety; the study

at Uncle Albert's house looking warm and friendly
and inviting; the professor beetle shouting rude
instructions at some little beetles that had got into
difficulty; again a glimpse of her uncle's study; then
a turnstile – one of those that only turn one way, so
once you have passed through it you can't get back;

playful light beams now shrieking with fear as they hurtle past the window to their destruction; walking up the down-escalator and not being able to get anywhere; yet another brief snatch of the study . . .

Why was that? Why did the study keep coming and going like that? In a flash, Gedanken realized what must be going on. It was Uncle Albert. He was trying to get her back. That was it. By the power of his imagination he was trying to do something that was physically impossible. He was trying to win her back from the greedy black hole – to release her from its iron grip and return her to the safety of the study.

'Come on, Uncle,' she muttered defiantly. 'I know you can do it.'

Just then there was an enormous explosion. A great tearing sound and the rocket section at the rear of the spacecraft pulled away. The walls of the craft crashed inwards, the air rushed out into the inky blackness.

'UNCLE! UNCLE!' she screamed.

The next thing she knew, Uncle Albert was shaking her and yelling into her face, 'You fool, you fool! You bloody, bloody little fool!'

She had never seen him in such a rage. In fact, in all the time she had known him, she had never heard him swear before. He must be absolutely mad with her. Normally it would have horrified her to think of him being so cross with her. But she loved it. Oh, how she loved it! What a relief! She was back, safe and sound. Anything, but *anything* was better

than what she had been through. She grabbed him
and hugged and hugged him.

'You were wonderful! Absolutely wonderful!' she
cried. 'You got me back. You beat the nasty black
hole. Thank you, thank you.' Then she looked at
him more closely. 'Why, Uncle, you're wet. You're
sweating all over.'

'What do you expect?' he demanded.

'You'd better sit down,' she suggested. She
settled him in his chair, and was relieved to see that
he seemed to be calming down a little. She sat
opposite him. There was an awkward silence. He
glared across at her.

'Well?' he said sternly. 'What have you to say for
yourself?'

Gedanken stared down at the carpet, unable to
look him in the eye.

'Can't imagine what got into you. Whyever did
you do it? It wasn't like you.'

'It was the star.'

'What star?'

'The star that went past the window. It fell
towards the hole, but then slowed down. It stopped
just outside the hole. At least, I thought it did. And I
reckoned that if a star got stopped at the edge, I'd be
safe, what with my rocket and all.'

'But it only *looked* as if it didn't go in,' said Uncle
Albert. 'It was just a trick of the light.'

Gedanken was puzzled. 'How do you mean – a
trick of the light?'

'Well, *think* about it. As the star got closer to the

hole, gravity got stronger. It was harder for the light to drag itself away, so it took longer to get to you. As the star got to the very outskirts of the hole, its light could hardly move at all at first. It had to inch its way bit by bit towards you . . .'

'Like you in the rowing boat. When you were close to the weir – you had to row hard but didn't move much.'

'Of course. The light speeded up as it got closer to you, but took ages to do the first part of the journey. That's why it took a long time for the light to get to you.'

'It got worn out?'

Uncle Albert nodded. 'Yes, sort of. And the light given out as the star crossed the boundary itself took for ever to get to you. So that's why the star seemed to get stuck.'

'But it didn't actually get stuck?' she asked.

'Not at all. It did the same as you did. Went straight on in. Didn't slow down. Just fell faster and faster. It's only to someone outside the black hole that it *appears* to stop.'

'I see,' muttered Gedanken. 'But I still don't understand where the boundary was. I didn't see it at all. Then suddenly Dick's telling me I've passed it.'

'There wasn't anything to see. The closer in you get, the stronger the gravity. At some point it gets too strong for even light to escape. But there's no signpost or anything to warn you that you've got there.'

'How sneaky! Black holes are really horrid, aren't they? By the way, Uncle,' she added, 'how did you know that we'd gone in? Did you get a message from Dick, or something?'

He shook his head. 'No. One moment you were parked outside the hole with your engines on. I started examining the material falling towards the hole – the way it was being captured. When I looked again, you'd gone. I searched. Couldn't find you. There was only one place you could be – inside. That's when I started trying to get you back; I knew I hadn't got long to do it.'

'And if you hadn't got me out in time?'

'Doesn't bear thinking about. You'd have been crushed to a point. Everything going into the hole – dust clouds, light beams, stars, spacecraft, you – anything crossing the boundary sphere marking the edge of the hole – it gets crushed out of existence when it arrives at the central point of the hole.'

'I'd have been completely wrecked!' Gedanken exclaimed in horror.

'You sure would.'

'But how come I felt *stretched*? I was being crushed at the sides but my feet felt they were being *pulled*.'

'That's because gravity gets stronger the closer you are to that central point. You were falling feet first, so your feet were closer in than the rest of your body. That means they were being pulled harder than the rest of you. So you got stretched in that direction. But eventually the whole of your body lands up at the central point – so everything in the end gets crushed.'

'Oh dear, I've just had a thought,' said Gedanken unhappily. 'Is that what happened to Dick?'

'Afraid so. But,' added Uncle Albert with a grin, 'I shouldn't worry. Dick was part of the imaginary world of the thought-bubble. I can always imagine him back again if I want to. The tricky bit was getting *you* back to where *you* belong – in the real world.'

Gedanken felt happier. 'Tell me, Uncle, what happens to everything after it's been squashed down?'

'Who knows? Perhaps it goes through a tunnel and squirts itself out into another universe somewhere else. There's no way of telling.'

Gedanken remembered the tunnel along which she had to pass to get to the Imaginary Universes Laboratory. 'Could we end up with the beetles – in their two-dimensional universe?'

Uncle Albert laughed.

'One more thing,' said Gedanken. 'I've just thought. You know how acceleration can fake gravity – the Big Dipper Principle and all that? Well, gravity was stretching me one way – in the direction pointing to the centre of the hole – and crushing me in the sideways direction, right? How can acceleration fake *that*?'

'Hmmm, that's a good point. It can't. Acceleration can only fake gravity when the gravity is the same everywhere – equally strong and pulling in the same direction – like it is in this room, more or less. But it can't fake it when it varies from one place to another.'

'So the Principle's no good after all.'

'Hey, I didn't say that. It's the Principle that got us started on all this in the first place, remember. No, the Principle is fine – provided you use it – as I said – over a region where gravity is more or less the same.'

Gedanken got up to go home. She thanked him once again, saying she now felt better about going on the radio. 'And, hey, I almost forgot,' she added. 'We've found a new lead guitar. We're forming this new band, and guess what it's called – Galactic Outbursts! Great name, don't you think? I've told the others I'm going to get Chris Parker to give it a plug.'

Uncle Albert looked doubtful. 'Well, all I can say is let's hope you can cut out the squabbling long enough . . .' His voice trailed off. He looked around as though he had lost something.

'What is it, Uncle?' Gedanken asked.

'The bag. The shopping bag. Where did you put it?'

'Er, in the hall – I think. By the front door.'

'Oh no,' said Uncle Albert. 'The ice-cream!'

# 8  What It Was All About

'Gedanken? Hello. I'm Susan. Would you like to come this way.'

'Am I late?' Gedanken asked anxiously.

The lady smiled. 'No. Everything's fine.'

They got to a door labelled 'Studio 1', and went in. The room had a large glass window panel at the far end, looking into the studio itself. And there, sitting at the control desk with earphones on, was Chris Parker. Gedanken recognized him from photographs. His voice could be heard over a loud-speaker. He was interviewing a boy – something to do with pet frogs. They were laughing away, having a great time.

'Am I on next?' she mouthed silently, not daring to make a sound.

'No need to whisper. They can't hear us. They're sound-proofed,' said Susan.

It was a bit like the Imaginary Universes Laboratory, thought Gedanken. You could hear them, but they couldn't hear you.

'Yes, you're on next,' Susan continued.

Gedanken felt awful. Pet frogs. She wished she hadn't come.

'Not getting nervous, are you?' asked Susan.

'A bit.'

'No need. Everyone will be so envious of you.'

'They won't.'

'Of course they will. I am for a start.'

'You?' exclaimed Gedanken. 'But you work for Chris Parker.'

Susan didn't reply – just shrugged her shoulders.

They listened to the end of the boy's interview, then the next record began playing.

'That's it. You're on,' said Susan, leading the way through to the studio next door. Gedanken had to sit in a seat opposite Chris Parker. He looked across, smiled, winked at her, and said 'Hi there . . . er . . .' He glanced down at a sheet in front of him. '. . . Gedanken. Unusual name. How do you pronounce it? "G" as in "get" or as in "German"?'

'Er, "get" please.'

'Be with you in a moment.' He swivelled round to set up the next track. 'Still raining outside? Can't tell in here.'

'Umm. I think so. No, I think it's stopped. I'm not sure,' she said nervously.

He didn't seem to hear. He was busy with other things. Turning back, he quickly scanned the sheet again, looked up at the clock, and reached forward to slide a knob towards himself, at the same time sliding another away with the other hand – presumably fading out the music. He began talking in his familiar rapid-fire voice.

'And that was the latest sound from the Big Mac

131

Boys. Radio Beacon, 92.6 FM. The Chris Parker Tuesday Show, calling all teenagers. The time is just coming up to twenty-one minutes past seven o'clock. Tonight we are certainly – *hopping* – from one subject to another. From frogs to physics. Oh no, I hear you say. Yawn, yawn. Boring. Not so. I have in the studio the world's youngest scientist – at least I reckon she must be. Yes, that's right, I said "she". Our next guest is Gedanken. Welcome to the show. I should explain, listeners, that Gedanken works with her Uncle Albert, the world-famous scientist. Not for her parties and discos. Every evening after school and at weekends she's hard at it doing research. That's what I said: *research*!'

Gedanken was about to protest that she *did* go to

discos and parties, and it was no big deal being a girl doing physics, but before she could open her mouth, there came the first question.

'Now, Gedanken, when I hear the words "big bang" I think of the noise that ends a firework display, but I believe you and your uncle have discovered another type of Big Bang. Tell us about it.'

She swallowed hard and began, 'Well, the Big Bang happened a long time ago. It was a gigantic explosion that went very wrong and created the Universe . . .'

Thud!

'Oh no,' thought Gedanken. 'Not another.'

She recognized the large brown envelope on the door mat with 'RADIO BEACON' printed across the top. Yet more listeners' letters being forwarded to her.

The interview had been a mess. She had actually cried when she got home. Chris Parker never gave her enough time to explain anything properly. He kept on butting in with silly comments. She was cross at the way he had treated her as though she weren't a normal girl – some kind of freak. And she hated him calling her 'Professor Gedanken'. He obviously thought he was being funny, but he wasn't. Then towards the end she had lost her temper completely and declared that if the listeners wanted to find out what it was really all about, they had better write to her. Never for one moment did she imagine they would! Now all this. And she *hated* having to write letters. It was letter-writing that spoiled Christmas and birthdays. Not only that, but she had been so upset, she had clean forgotten to plug Galactic Outbursts. Not so much as a mention. She felt she had made a right fool of herself. 'No boy's ever going to ask me out again after that,' she thought miserably to herself. Mind you, Jeremy had been very nice to her. She had met him in the street. She had tried to avoid him because she was so embarrassed. Besides, she expected he would still be sulking about the break-up of his band. But he had crossed the road – actually crossed the road – to tell her he thought it was the most interesting interview he had ever heard on the Parker Show. Just shows you can't tell. She always did think Jeremy was all right – once you got to know him.

On arriving at Uncle Albert's, she scattered the latest batch of letters across his kitchen table. 'Well,' she said. 'What am I going to do with this lot? Haven't even *started* answering the pile I got yesterday.'

Uncle Albert grinned. 'Don't blame me. It's the price of fame. You'll have to get used to this sort of thing if you're going to be a pop star. Pop stars get a hundred times that many fan letters – every day.'

'They do? How do they manage? Do they just throw them away?'

'Shouldn't think so. Probably pay people to answer them.'

'Really? That sounds good,' she said, adding, 'Heh. Come to think of it, that *is* a good idea. You could help me now. How about you answering this lot for me?' She slid a batch across the table to him.

'I said they get *paid* for it,' replied Uncle Albert.

'Oh.'

'Actually, I'm not doing anything special this morning. Suppose I could lend a hand. Could be quite a useful way of revising what we've learned.'

'That's great!' exclaimed Gedanken.

'Mind you, you'll have to write out the replies yourself in your own handwriting and in your own words – they'll expect it to come from you.'

'Oh,' said Gedanken, looking a little disappointed. 'I was hoping . . . But, I suppose you're right. Still, it'll help if I can check out my answers against yours – to make sure I've got them right. When do you want to do it?'

'Now.'

'NOW!' she protested.

Uncle Albert pointed sternly to the chair opposite him. He took out pencil and paper and began looking through the letters. He numbered the questions, and jotted down the answers on a separate sheet.

These are the questions:

1. 'Suppose I carry a ruler to the top of a skyscraper on a very heavy planet, and I'm holding it vertically. It would end up longer than when it started, right? Does that mean that as I am going up in the lift, I see it expanding?'

2. 'I am writing this letter while being kept in after

school. I'm bored. I can't wait for the teacher's watch to say 4.30 so I can go home. If gravity was strong, I could go to the top floor of the building and speed up my time. That way the teacher's watch down here would appear to go faster, and it wouldn't seem so long. Yes?'

3. 'I go to school by train. As the train gets up speed, does the driver's watch run faster, slower, or the same as that of the guard travelling in the last carriage? Secondly, how do their watches compare as the train slows down?'

4. 'If you wanted to find out how an astronaut's body was likely to stand up to the strain of living on a very, very heavy planet, is there some way of testing it before actually visiting the planet?'

5. 'When a light beam from a distant star passes close by the rim of the Sun on its journey to us, is it affected by the Sun's gravity? If so, how?'

6. 'If the Universe is the sort where an astronaut can do a round trip in a straight line, it has no edge or boundary (like the balloon for the two-dimensional beetles). Does that mean it has an infinite number of galaxies?'

7. 'I liked the idea of the Universe being like the "balloon" type of universe for the beetles. Suppose the Universe really was like that, and you had *two* astronauts leaving the Earth at the same time in opposite directions, one from the North Pole, the other from the South. They both do the round trip in straight lines at the same

speed, so they get back together. At the half-way point of their journeys, are they at their furthest point from the Earth? Are they then furthest from each other?'

8. 'I found the rubber sheet universe really useful for understanding things better. Is there anything in that universe that would be like a black hole to a beetle?'

9. 'Did you say that a black hole is left when an old planet collapses in on itself?'

10. 'This black hole business has got me worried. Is there any danger of the Sun becoming a black hole?'

11. 'You said that if you drop a clock into a black hole, and you watch it from a long way off, the hands appear to go round slower the closer it gets to the hole. When do the hands appear to stop – before reaching the boundary of the hole, or at the boundary exactly, or when it is crushed to a point at the centre of the hole?'

12. 'If you were falling into the black hole *with* the clock, when would the hands appear to stop?'

13. 'You tried to get out of the black hole with an ordinary rocket. But suppose your spacecraft had a two-stage rocket. Once the first stage had used up its fuel you leave it behind so you're not having to push the empty casing. Could you then have got out of the black hole with the remaining extra stage?'

14. 'Why was the rocket section of Gedanken's craft pulled off rather than crushed?'

Having finished writing his answers, Uncle Albert popped them into an envelope. He stuck it down, and handed it to Gedanken.

'I suggest you try having a go at answering the questions yourself first,' he said. 'You can then compare your answers with mine.'

With that he started putting on the shabby jacket he always kept hanging on the hook on the back door.

'Where are you going?' asked Gedanken.

'We never did finish that weeding, did we? I'm about to change into a monster and terrorize the little people in the garden. With any luck, might find a beetle to squash – provided, of course,' he added with a wink, 'it wears a white coat and shouts a lot.'

## UNCLE ALBERT'S ANSWERS

1. Wherever you are – at the top of the building, at the bottom, or in between – what you have with you looks its normal size. This is because not only does the ruler get bigger as you go up, but also the size of your eyes. The picture of the ruler on the screen at the back of your eye is bigger, but so is the screen – in the same ratio. So the answer is no.

2. Good try – but you got it the wrong way round! You need to send your teacher to the top of the building so as to speed up his watch. You stay below.

3. While the train is accelerating, the driver's watch at the front goes faster than the guard's. Slowing down, the equivalent gravity pulls the opposite way to what it did when speeding up. (If you're standing, you tend to fall towards the front rather than the back of the train now.) So that means it is the turn of the guard's watch to go faster than the driver's.

4. Yes. You make him accelerate very, very hard.

5. Yes. It is slightly pulled towards the Sun so changes direction a little.

6. No. There would be a finite number – you would be able to count them all. To see why, think of the two-dimensional rubber balloon universe with pebbles stuck to it to represent the galaxies. To a beetle crawling over the surface there is no edge or boundary, but there is

only a finite number of pebbles. As it crawls round and round in circles it keeps revisiting the same pebbles. To have an infinite number of pebbles you'd have to have a rubber sheet that was more or less flat and just went on and on for ever. Our universe might be like that – it might have an infinite number of galaxies – but if so, it will have to go on for ever in all directions and wouldn't be the sort where an astronaut could do a round trip in a straight line.

7. Think of the two-dimensional rubber balloon universe. Two beetles start off from the same point in opposite directions. Half-way through their round trips, they are both directly opposite their starting point. They are, therefore, at their furthest distance from the starting point, but they are not furthest from each other – they are at the same place! The same will be true of your astronauts.

8. Yes. Just think of a very heavy pebble making a very steep-sided dimple – and a poor little beetle struggling to get out of it, but slithering deeper and deeper into it.

9. No. It was a *star* that collapsed, not a planet.

10. Only very heavy stars have enough matter to produce the very strong gravity of a black hole. The Sun has *not* got enough, so there's no danger.

11. The hands appear to stop when the clock gets to the boundary.

12. Falling into the black hole with the clock, time

seems to pass normally. The clock keeps going as usual even as you go through the boundary. It only stops when it (and you!) are crushed out of existence at the central point of the hole (or a little earlier when the stretching and crushing forces wreck it).

13. Using a two-stage rocket makes no difference. Gedanken's rocket was already delivering all the power one could possibly imagine, and it still wasn't enough. Once in a black hole, there is no way – but *no* way – of getting out.

14. The same reason as Gedanken felt her feet being pulled off. The rocket motors were closer to the centre of the hole than the rest of the craft (it was falling in backwards, remember) so was experiencing a stronger gravitational pull than the rest of the craft.

# 9 P.S. A Bit of Real Science

The story you have just read was, of course, a made-up one. But the nature of space, time, and gravity really is as remarkable as you have now learned.

The Universe actually did begin with a Big Bang. The galaxies are still flying apart as space continues to expand and carry them along with it. As for black holes, though we cannot be absolutely sure yet, it does now seem that they exist. They are formed from very heavy stars. Also, some galaxies appear to have a black hole at their centre – a hole that swallows up all the stars that come near it.

Gravity bends light. Because of the Sun's gravity, light beams from a distant star will change direction. When the light is distorted in this way, the star looks as though it is in the wrong position in the sky. Gravity affects time. It causes a clock on the ground to run more slowly than an identical one placed at high altitude. This has been checked using clocks on aircraft. When light coming from the top of a tall building is examined very carefully at ground level, its colour is found to be bluer than normal – another effect of gravity. As for distances being longer when you are close in to a star, this is also the case. It shows up, for instance, when working out the path followed by Mercury – the planet most affected because it passes closest to the Sun.

Space behaves as though it has an overall curvature. Whether it is so curved that it closes in on itself (like a balloon), thus making it possible to do a round trip of the Universe in a straight line, we simply don't know. The thrill of one day making that discovery belongs to a scientist who is probably still at school now – *your* school, perhaps; it might even be *you*!

These interesting ideas arise out of something called The General Theory of Relativity. The theory is based on the same Equivalence Principle you have just read about. It was first suggested by one of the world's most famous scientists, Albert Einstein, in 1907. He once said of this discovery:

'The happiest thought of my life. I was sitting in a chair when all of a sudden a thought occurred to me: if a person falls freely he will not feel his own weight. I was startled. This simple thought made a deep impression on me.'

It was this thought that started Einstein on the road to his theory of gravity – still the most beautiful way of organizing how we think about the Universe.

Einstein got very excited about his work. When he found that his theory exactly predicted the path of Mercury, he was beside himself with happiness for days. The result showed that the curvature idea was not just a different way of looking at gravity from the old one, but a *better* way.

He was a lovable, eccentric man. (He *did* play the violin, and *didn't* wear socks!) Though some people found him rather wrapped up in his thoughts, he always enjoyed talking to children about science. Children, he found, shared his own sense of wonder about the world.

Einstein is the all-time hero of those who explore science at its deepest, most mysterious level – the level known as 'physics'. Many physicists (pronounced 'fizzy-sists') have large pictures of him on the walls of their laboratories – just as you might have pictures of your favourite pop stars on the walls of your bedroom at home.

In his work, he relied on his amazing sense of imagination. He would dream up all kinds of possibilities – like beetles crawling over different shaped surfaces, and someone being shut up in a box in outer space trying to find out whether he was accelerating or being acted upon by gravity – and would then test out these ideas to see if they had anything to say about the real world. This use of his imagination came to be known as his 'thought' experiments, or in his native German language, 'gedanken' experiments.

He was a modest man:

'When the blind beetle crawls over the surface of a globe, he doesn't notice that the track he has covered is curved. I was lucky enough to have spotted it.'

Just luck? Surely not. It takes genius to go from

playful thoughts about beetles to a deep understanding of the Universe. Not that his cleverness
was always recognized. When at school, he was
bored. So much so, he was thought to be backward.
'Could not be expected to make a success of anything,' his teacher once said of him. Make a note of
that. Could come in handy next time your parents
talk to your teacher about you.

If you enjoyed this story, be sure not to miss

# THE TIME AND SPACE OF UNCLE ALBERT

This is the best-selling first book in Russell Stannard's Uncle Albert series. Join Gedanken and Dick as they try to break the ultimate speed barrier. Follow their adventures as they make further astonishing discoveries about the mysteries of time and space – how going fast makes you: put on weight without getting fat; flattens you without it hurting; helps you to live for ever without knowing it. All these effects, like the ones you have just learned about, are true – they come from Einstein's *Special* Theory of Relativity.

*The Time and Space of Uncle Albert* was shortlisted for both the Whitbread Children's Novel 1989, and the under-fourteen Science Book Prize 1989.

'This is no ordinary children's book' *Daily Mail*
'A superb read' *Times Educational Supplement*
'Unique' *Guardian*
'An extraordinary book' *Good Housekeeping*
'Entertaining, ingenious, stimulating' *School Science Review*
'I couldn't put this book down' *Physics Education*
'Exciting, accessible, refreshing, genuine' *Physics World*